Out of Their Minds

Read more about Lenora and Coren in these other "Minds" books by Carol Matas and Perry Nodelman

Of Two Minds
More Minds

Out of Their Minds

Carol Matas and Perry Nodelman

Simon & Schuster Books for Young Readers

SIMON & SCHUSTER BOOKS FOR YOUNG READERS
An imprint of Simon & Schuster Children's Publishing Division
1230 Avenue of the Americas
New York, New York 10020

Text copyright © 1998 by Carol Matas and Perry Nodelman

SIMON & SCHUSTER BOOKS FOR YOUNG READERS is a trademark of Simon & Schuster.
Book design by Jennifer Reyes
The text for this book is set in Goudy.
Printed in the United States of America
First Edition
10 9 8 7 6 5 4 3 2 1
Library of Congress Cataloging-in-Publication Data
Matas, Carol, 1949-
Out of their minds / Carol Matas and Perry Nodelman.
p. cm.
Sequel to: Of two minds and More minds.
Summary: About to be married in Coren's homeland of Andilla, Coren and Lenora
discover that before the wedding can proceed they must find out why the Andillan people
have lost their special powers and why Lenora is having nightmares about the evil Hevak.
ISBN 0-689-81946-3
[1. Psychic ability—Fiction. 2. Fantasy.] I. Nodelman, Perry. II. Title.
PZ7.M423964Ou 1998
[Fic]—dc21
97-41277

FIRST
F
EDITION

For Peter Atwood—out of his, too.

Out of Their Minds

CHAPTER 1

*I*t is gray. Gray sky, gray mist, gray under foot. She is alone.

She calls out, but her voice is swallowed up, lost in the thick mists. She shivers. Where is she? How did she get here? Where is everyone else?

Suddenly, a voice cuts through the fog. Not hers. Someone else's voice, sharp, strong, clear.

"Lenora!" it calls. "Lenora!"

Her stomach twists. She knows that voice.

"Come to me, Lenora," the voice entreats her. "We belong together. You know we do."

The voice is compelling, dangerous, evil. Where is Coren? He should be here to help her. But he's not. She is alone, alone with the voice.

"Lenora. Come to me."

It is tempting, very tempting.

She begins to move forward. One step. Then another. She knows that if she reaches the voice, it could mean the end of her. But she can't stop herself. She takes another step, and another, and—

"Ouch!" Lenora sat up with a start. She looked around. For a moment, she was still inside her nightmare and she couldn't place where she actually was. It was gray here, but not the misty gray of the dream—darker, murkier. She could just barely make out objects in the dim light—people, it looked like, human bodies hanging from trees or rafters. Dead bodies, corpses!

No, she realized with relief, not corpses at all. Just empty clothing, her own traveling outfit and Coren's and the Keeper Agneth's, hanging from the poles of the cramped tent the three of them were sleeping in.

She was in a tent. Dawn was breaking. Of course. She was in the mountains in a tent at dawn, traveling with Coren and Agneth. They were heading to Andilla, Coren's homeland. She and Coren would finally be married there.

Agneth had insisted that the wedding be held in Andilla. It had to do with a silly rule in The Precious Recordings, the ancient sacred books that laid out the rules of the Balance. You would unbalance a chapel forever, apparently, if you tried to marry the same people in it more than once. The Balance just wouldn't stand for it. And that meant that, after their earlier unsuccessful attempt at a wedding, the chapel back home in Gepeth was out.

Lenora remembered how bitterly her father and mother had complained. King Rayden wanted the wedding in *his* castle in *his* country where everyone would be *his* guests and have to listen to *his* jokes. Queen Savet hated to think about how dusty the castle would get and how sloppily the towels would be folded while she was away in Andilla and unable to supervise everything properly. And to have a wedding there, in Andilla, where people lived inside their own imagined thoughts and ignored the real world around them . . .

Finally, of course, the Keeper decided, and the Balance won. The entire Gepethian court packed up their fancy wedding clothes and then spent the entire trip arguing about whether or not to imagine away the horrible bumps in the rarely used road. After all, all Gepethians had the ability to make what they imagined real—not just real inside their own minds, as was the case with the Andillans, but in actual living fact. But unlike the Andillans, the Gepethians rarely used their ability. They agreed on one reality and stuck to it. For the most part—Lenora would have smoothed over the bumps in the road without a second thought. But for everyone else it was a big decision. Had the Keeper been with them the answer would, naturally, have been no—it could upset the Balance. But even if he wasn't there, nobody actually had the nerve to change things. The nobility's backsides were getting increasingly sore as they moved east over the mountains toward Andilla in a long train of horses and coaches and wagons full of wedding gifts and other gifts for their Andillan hosts and host-esses, arguing all the way.

Agneth meanwhile, was occupied elsewhere. He, Coren, and Lenora herself had left the Gepeth court a week or so earlier than the rest. Before heading through the mountain passes and on to Andilla, they had a side trip to make.

Back before their first attempt to marry, Lenora's parents had promised Lenora and Coren a home on the island of Crosnor as a wedding gift. Now that the wedding was finally happening, they needed to see the house there, and to make plans for the life they would live in it. Agneth had accompanied them at his own insistence.

"I can just imagine what dangerous mischief you two would get into on your own," harrumphed Agneth. "Why, before anybody could stop you, Crosnor would have turned into—oh, I don't know. A mound of ice cream floating on a sea of custard, maybe."

"Hmm," said Coren mischievously. "Not a bad idea, Agneth."

"Not bad at all," Lenora agreed. "You're getting surprisingly imaginative these days, Agneth. Let's hope the International Brotherhood of Keepers doesn't hear about it."

Agneth, exasperated, said nothing, just stared at them, then shook his head and stomped off. The Keeper was all too easy to tease—it was hardly even any fun..

Crosnor had turned out to be everything that Lenora and Coren had hoped. Lenora smiled to herself in the darkness of the tent as she thought about it.

The house was a simple little cottage—just big enough for the two them, not even any servants' quarters. And the island itself was separated from the mainland by a vast gulf, miles from anywhere and anybody. They would be totally and completely alone there—free to do just as they pleased.

The best thing about it, Lenora thought—next to being with Coren, of course—was that she could get on with her plan of experimenting with ways to make the world a better place. During the adventures she'd been having recently, she had learned things about life in Gepeth and elsewhere that deeply distressed her. The Balance might be good for some people, but everywhere she visited there was always somebody who had to suffer for it. She wanted happiness and justice for everybody and she was going to make sure it happened, no matter what. Surely there could be a world where good triumphed and everyone loved everyone else?

But first, of course, she had to figure out what that would be like—to imagine a perfect and perfectly good world. Once she and Coren were safely married and back on Crosnor, she could imagine anything and everything she wanted and nobody would even know.

Especially not Agneth. The pompous old fool had taken one look at the island and announced his intention to have King Rayden keep fifty of the strongest minds of Gepeth permanently posted on the mainland just across the strait from Crosnor to make sure things didn't get out of hand. But Lenora couldn't leave her powers unused as they wanted her to do—why, it would be practically criminal. After all, if she could imagine things and then make what she imagined real, then she had a duty to do it!

Hah, Lenora thought as she stared into the gloom of the tent. Agneth thinks he can stop me, does he? We'll see about that.

Lenora put her hand to her brow. Sopping wet. What an awful dream.

Coren, still fast asleep on the mat beside hers, turned over and kicked out, barely missing her. What a restless sleeper he was—always worrying, even when he wasn't awake. Being close to him while he was asleep was an invitation to jabs and bruises.

Well, at least she knew what had wakened her from the dream. As she herself slept, she must have rolled off her own mat in his direction and into the range of his flailing. As usual, she didn't know whether to kick him back or kiss him. So, after checking to make sure the Keeper was sound enough asleep not to notice, she did both.

"Ouch!" Coren protested. Then, "Oh!"

The "oh" was for the kiss. He looked up at her, bewildered, rubbing the sleep out of his eyes. "What did I do to deserve that?"

"Shush," Lenora whispered, pointing over her shoulder in the direction of Agneth. Coren looked over at the Keeper, who was snoring loudly not very far away from them, and nodded.

"You kicked me in your sleep," she went on, "so I kicked you back. But the kick woke me from a horrible nightmare. That's why I kissed you."

Coren smiled and reached up for another kiss, which she gladly returned. Then, realizing what she'd said, he sat up on his mat. "You never have nightmares, Lenora, never."

It was true. Lenora was always so sure of herself, even in her sleep. It made Coren very envious. He himself always had nightmares. Why, just now he'd been having a horrible one about being attacked by a pack of angry, biting dogs, tiny dogs of every color of the rainbow—he'd been kicking out at them, but it wasn't having any effect on them at all. They just kept right on climbing up his legs. Thank goodness Lenora had awakened him.

But Lenora's own dreams were nothing like that. She was always telling Coren about some wonderful dream or other in which things worked out just the way she wanted them. They were adventure stories in which she single-handedly saved her parents from evil brigands or the entire world from invading alien forces. Or sometimes, she dreamed of magnificent schemes of vengeance directed at people who annoyed her. Her mother would be locked up in a very dusty room with a broom that moved away from her every time she reached out for it. Or her father would be standing in front of a vast throng, about to make a stirring speech, and he would discover that his mouth had suddenly disappeared and that there was nothing but skin between his nose and his chin. And as for what she dreamed about Coren himself whenever he made her angry—it made Coren shiver just thinking about it.

But she never had nightmares. And she'd just had a nightmare, she said. It was bound to mean something bad—something else for Coren to worry about. As if wondering if Agneth would wake up and start yelling at them weren't enough. Not to mention this whole business of actually finally getting married to Lenora. Not to mention the mere existence of Lenora.

"What exactly happened in this nightmare?" he asked her.

"I dreamed—" Lenora paused, looked ashamed. "I dreamed about Hevak," she finally muttered.

awake Keeper out of the tent so that she could get dressed, Coren decided to use his Andillan power of thought-reading to get in touch with his parents and let them know that they'd be in Andilla soon—once they left the mountains it was only a day's ride to the court. He knew from previous mind-to-mind conversations that his parents had been getting anxious, feeling overwhelmed by having to plan a wedding involving guests from other countries who wouldn't be able to share their mental pictures of the food and the decorations. If King Rayden and Queen Savet hadn't been there to help them out, it would have been a total disaster—and what with all the royal egos at work, things were pretty uneasy as it was.

Coren concentrated on his mother first, began to create a clear picture of her in his mind. She was the one who was most worried about the wedding plans, and he knew from previous mental conversations with her that she was desperately worried she'd end up with a houseful of wedding guests and no bride and groom. She'd be glad to hear they were so close.

Mother, he thought, Coren here. Can you hear me?

No answer. He tried again. Still nothing.

Well, maybe she was asleep still. But his father would be up for sure. For no reason anybody could figure out, King Arno, who'd never before in his entire life even stepped into a kitchen, had suddenly developed a fascination with baking— actual baking with real ingredients in a real kitchen, not just imaginary baking in the world of his mind—and he had decided to personally prepare all the breads and buns for the wedding celebrations.

This behavior worried Coren terribly. After all, no one in Andilla ever did anything real, not when they could just imagine it as being real inside their thoughts. Why wasn't his father simply imagining that he was baking?

"Hevak!" Coren tensed at the mere mention of the name. Of all the bad things that had ever happened to him, Hevak was the very worst. And it was all Lenora's fault—no wonder she was ashamed even to say his name.

Why would Lenora be dreaming about Hevak, of all things?

"But," he said, mostly to reassure himself, "it's really no surprise—I mean, after the way Agneth was going on and on about Hevak just last night."

It was true, Lenora thought. Before bed she had accidentally said something just a little too honest about the life she was planning to live on Crosnor and her scheme to imagine a perfectly good world, and Agneth had blown up at her, and then droned on and on about how foolhardy she was and about what a close call they'd all had the time she misused her powers and let Hevak loose. Well! She hadn't done it intentionally, after all! And just because Hevak almost took over the entire world, it wasn't *really* her fault. And anyway, she'd dealt with Hevak, hadn't she? So why was Agneth always reminding her about it?

"Agneth's tirade," Lenora agreed. "That's what I was thinking. But you know, Coren, it was so real. I was in the gray—remember, just like you were, probably, when Hevak sent you there?"

Coren remembered, all right. He wasn't likely to forget the time that Hevak had made him disappear. He shuddered.

"Well," he said, trying desperately to believe it himself, "thankfully, that's all behind us now. The scariest thing we have to look forward to is the wedding party." He leaned over and kissed Lenora once more, hoping that it was true. Somehow, when he was around Lenora, nothing was ever that simple.

A few minutes later, after Lenora sent him and the barely

Because he certainly wasn't. Coren was quite sure he'd find his father in the gleaming white, gadget-loaded kitchen Arno had persuaded his new friend King Rayden to imagine into existence for him, covered in flour and happily kneading dough.

Coren concentrated as hard as he could, but there was no answer from his father either. Both of his parents were unavailable.

And come to think of, he didn't get much sense of any sort of mental activity from the direction of Andilla. Were his own powers not working?

He focused his attention on the Keeper, who was standing on one leg a few feet away from Coren with a dark look on his face.

Blasted stocking, Coren heard Arno thinking. It was just here a minute ago. If I don't find it soon I'll have to put my bare foot down on the cold ground, or else all this obscene hopping on one leg will make the Balance suffer. Where is the blasted thing?

No, Coren thought as he planted a suggestion in the Keeper's mind to turn just to his left and look at the shrub from which Coren could see the tip of the missing stocking sticking out, *my* powers are okay. So why can't I reach Andilla?

Maybe it was some sort of surprise they were planning for him and Lenora. Yes, that made sense, sort of. They were planning a wedding surprise, some sort of gift, and they were masking their thoughts from him so he wouldn't find out about it. It was the only logical explanation. Wasn't it?

Well, there was no point in mentioning it to Lenora. Why should they both worry?

Still, he himself worried about it the whole time he ate his breakfast—a huge plate of hotcakes with butter and syrup that Lenora had made appear in place of the crusty pieces of hardtack Agneth had given them from the apparently endless supply he carried in his traveling bags. Coren had managed to distract the Keeper by suggesting that the trees around them somehow seemed different than they'd been the night before, more lopsided, sort of. Was it possible that something might have changed them—something to do with the Balance, perhaps? The Keeper, remembering his dangerous one-sock hopping, had immediately headed off to take a closer look at the trees, all the while muttering about his own thoughtless folly.

The hotcakes were delicious—much better than hardtack. Once more, Coren reminded himself of how lucky he was, really, to have Lenora and her wonderful imagination in his life. And tried not to worry too much.

They entered Andilla before nightfall. By then, Coren was a nervous wreck. He'd been trying, unsuccessfully, to reach his parents all day. It *had* to be a surprise. Didn't it?

For Lenora, everything she saw all day was a surprise. As they approached Coren's home, she couldn't help comparing it with the tidy green fields and neat cottages of the countryside back home in Gepeth. The contrast was remarkable. The Andillan countryside looked like a tornado had passed through some time ago and nobody had ever gotten around to cleaning up after it. The fields were filled with weeds and burrs that reached almost as high as their horses. The houses were disgusting unpainted hovels with broken glass in the windows and mud and broken pieces of furniture in the front yards.

Lenora knew, of course, that the people who lived in those hovels saw them as mansions. And because they imagined their houses as mansions, they lost consciousness of the horrible way they really looked.

But, Lenora reminded herself as they rode through the

mess, when Coren had lived in Andilla he had chosen not to use his powers. He'd been willing to view things as they actually were. Now, seeing the reality Coren had chosen to confront, Lenora could never again think of him as a coward.

"There it is," Coren said, pointing. "Home!"

On the road before them was a gate, and behind it, a vast palace.

Or more exactly, what used to be a palace. Parts of it, now, were merely heaps of fallen stone. In one place, a wall stood on its own, with no rooms left behind it and nothing but clear sky gleaming through its empty window frames. Even in the parts of the castle that stood intact there wasn't a single unbroken window.

Coren smiled happily and spurred his horse onward. It's true what they say, Lenora thought as she rushed off after him, leaving the Keeper in a cloud of dust. There's no place like home.

The minute their horses passed through the gate and into a rutted courtyard, they heard shouting.

"They're here," came voices from inside the palace. Then the huge front door on the other side of the courtyard burst open so quickly that it nearly flew off its one remaining hinge.

"Lenora!" Queen Savet shouted from the doorway. "Thank heavens you're finally here!"

"Yes, indeed," King Arno said, appearing behind her. "Yes, indeed!"

"It's a disaster," Queen Milda called to Coren as she pushed Lenora's parents aside and hurried down the stairs, almost putting her foot through one of the holes where a board was missing. "A total disaster!"

Nope, Lenora thought, surveying the group of hysterical parents that was rushing toward them, no place like home.

CHAPTER 2

"Coren," Queen Milda cried. "It's horrible!!"

"Mother, mother, please, calm down," said Coren as he leaped off his horse. Meanwhile, Queen Savet had grabbed on to Lenora's riding boot, still in the stirrup, and was yanking at her leg.

"Lenora!" Queen Savet announced. "It's horrible."

"Truly horrible," King Rayden added, rushing up to the other side of the horse and grabbing Lenora's other boot. "Something must be done!"

While Lenora's parents pulled her in opposite directions and Coren tried to calm his horse, the three monarchs kept right on talking. It seemed to have something to do with a sore throat and towels and too many dinner rolls—Lenora was too busy being almost ripped apart to pay all that much attention.

Meanwhile, Coren's horse was almost beyond his control, rearing up and kicking out its hooves in the direction of various parental body parts. There was no choice—Coren had to use his powers to try to calm it.

Stand! he thought. Just stand quietly and stop that silly neighing, right now!

As one, the horse, King Rayden, and the two queens stopped in mid-gesture. All four stood there in dead silence, staring at Coren. The horse looked the least surprised of the lot of them.

"Well," Queen Milda finally said. "I suppose this poor old

voice of mine does sound a little like neighing. But really, Coren, it wasn't very polite of you to mention it. The point is," she continued, "I can't hear anyone! Nor can anyone else— we've lost our powers! We all have to *speak*. *Aloud!*"

And indeed, Coren, realized, she *was* speaking aloud. And, come to think of it, it did sort of sound like a horse neighing. Like everyone else in Andilla, his mother never used her speaking voice when sending out a thought would do the trick. Her voice was creaky from a lifetime of disuse.

A sudden thought hit him. "Then how did you hear me when I spoke to that horse?"

"I don't know, Coren," she said mournfully. "Every once in a while something seems to get through."

"Thirteen cups of flour and six tablespoons of baking powder!" said an enthusiastic voice in Coren's head. His father's voice. "Perfect!" it added. "And now we sift!"

"Like that, for instance," Queen Milda said. "Honestly, Coren. I don't know what to do. Disaster strikes just when all this company is coming, and your father doesn't even seem to care. I can't get him out of that kitchen long enough to even talk about it! And if that wasn't bad enough, Coren, that future mother-in-law of yours over there"—she glanced over at Savet—"is driving me crazy. The world is coming to an end and all she can talk about is towels!"

Meanwhile, Lenora was huddled with her parents across the courtyard, talking about towels.

"There isn't one clean towel in the entire castle," said Queen Savet, "and hundreds of wedding guests on their way even as we speak! These people are living in squalor, absolute squalor, Lenora. Just thinking about it makes me feel quite faint."

King Rayden agreed. "I was happy to offer our assistance to

Coren's parents to fix the place up before the rest of the guests arrive—and this palace could certainly do with a bit of good old Gepethian imagination, no question about it. But that was before I actually saw the extent of the damage—it's beyond my powers, and you know my powers are considerable. I've managed a kitchen for Arno. And I did fix up a few nice rooms for your mother and me, of course—I won't sleep on a moldy mattress, and that's that."

"And the sheets, Lenora," Savet wailed. "The sheets they actually had the nerve to give us! Holes as big as my hand! We *had* to do it, didn't we? Didn't we?"

Queen Savet hated to use her powers, even when the sheets had holes in them—she was a devout believer in the Balance as it was and things as they already were. Lenora squeezed her mother's hand and nodded at her reassuringly.

King Rayden patted his wife on her back. "The rest of the palace is a total disaster. Agneth will have a fit when he sees it. Imagining this place into good enough shape for a wedding is going to put a serious stress on the Balance, no question about it. It'll take all sorts of complicated calculations and delicate adjustments."

"I'm surprised at you, Rayden," Queen Savet said. "Agneth will never allow you to fiddle with the Balance like that. He'll tell us to call in the carpenters, just as I suggested in the first place."

"As I told you, dearest," said Rayden patiently, "there *are* no carpenters in Andilla. I did try to ask the Keeper who lives here, Kaylor, about what to do. She's called Thoughtwatcher, not Keeper, but it amounts to the same thing. But apparently they're having some crisis or other of their own—something about the way they think, I'm not exactly sure because they're all too hysterical about it to bother to tell me clearly."

"Too hysterical is right, Lenora," Savet sniffed. "Your future mother-in-law can't even think clearly enough to find me a broom. She just goes around wailing in that awful croak of a voice she has. And as for Arno—well! The poor deluded man uses way too much baking powder in his dinner rolls! They'll be far too light if you ask me!"

"And," Rayden said, "dinner rolls are all *he* ever thinks about. I ask him about this crisis, and all he says is, 'Crisis? What crisis? Put these cookies in the oven.' And he calls himself a king! Hah! And meanwhile, the Thoughtwatcher is off somewhere or other reading the old books and praying for guidance and won't be interrupted. We need Agneth. Where *is* he, anyway?"

"Yes," Savet said. "Where is he? Those guests will start showing up any minute now! We'll be disgraced in front of the entire known universe!"

CHAPTER 3

After managing to calm their parents down a little—enough to get them back inside the castle—Lenora and Coren consulted with each other about what they'd heard. One thing was perfectly clear. Their parents were too busy worrying about their own problems to figure out why the others were upset. And none of the problems was going to get solved until they all pitched in and worked on them together. The first thing to do, then, was to get everyone to sit down in one room and actually pay attention to one another.

Lenora shepherded her parents toward the royal throne room, patiently pretending to listen as Savet pointed out every water stain on the wallpaper and all the holes the mice had gnawed through the brocade hangings. Coren sent his mother off to the kitchen to bully his father into joining them, while he himself went to find Kaylor, the Thoughtwatcher.

He knew exactly where to look. Back in the days when he was the only Andillan who didn't live in his mind, everyone else had been so busy with their own thoughts that they'd totally ignored him, and left him free to roam the palace as he wished. He knew every filthy nook and dilapidated cranny—including the Inner Temple of the Thoughtwatcher, a small room behind the chapel that was filled with old books and dusty papers. Indeed, Coren had once tried to read some of those books—and would have, too, if the language in them had not been so archaic and hard to follow.

Sure enough, Kaylor was there, madly flipping through the books and tossing them over her shoulder, with so much vigor you'd never guess she must be a hundred years old if she was a day.

As Coren came through the door, she gave him a withering glance. "Humph," she said in a voice just as creaky as Queen Milda's. "I might have known *you'd* be around when something like this happens." Kaylor had never approved of Coren's refusal to live inside his mind. Indeed, she'd once actually threatened to have him thrown into jail for it. There was an old Andillan statute, long since forgotten by everyone else, that said it was against the law to accept reality as it was, and Kaylor wanted to use it to teach Coren a lesson. She figured a few days in a moldy dungeon on bread and water would do the trick.

"If he wants reality," Kaylor had told King Arno, "let's give him reality." Fortunately, the offer of marriage had arrived from Gepeth just in time to save Coren from a bad week alone in the dark.

Now Kaylor looked as if she'd cheerfully throw him into that same dungeon again. It took him some time to persuade her that what was happening wasn't his fault—at least not as far as he knew. He himself had been trying to read minds also, he told her, without any luck. Except for that one outburst of his father's, he hadn't heard a single mental peep out of anybody since he'd arrived at the palace.

It was, in fact, more than a little distressing. As much as Coren disliked using his powers, it was strange to be in Andilla and not have the thoughts of other people buzzing uncontrollably through his mind. It just didn't seem right. What could be causing it? Some kind of interference or other? Some effect of the weather?

"I'm as worried about this as you are, Kaylor," he said as he walked with the bent old lady back to the throne room, holding her fragile arm to help her negotiate the small bumps where the carpet had lifted up from the floor. The look she gave him suggested she was as ready to believe that as she was to give up thoughtwatching and become a tightrope artist in a traveling circus. But at least she was willing to fill him in on recent events.

As he listened to Kaylor talk about what was happening, Coren began to worry even more. He hadn't realized how serious the situation was. It wasn't just that the Andillans in the court had lost their ability to read each other's minds. They'd lost all their other powers, too—especially the one they depended on the most, the ability to live in their imagination.

"Look at this place," Kaylor said to Coren, a tear actually trickling down her leathery cheek. "Our castle is a dump."

The surprising thing was not that the castle looked like a dump—for Coren it had always looked like a dump, ever since he had refused to think about it being any different than it really was. The surprising thing was that Kaylor also knew it looked like a dump—that, in fact, she couldn't imagine it looking like anything else, no matter how hard she thought about it. The spider webs and the threadbare patches in the carpet simply refused to go away.

And the same thing had happened to everyone in the entire court. The wonderful places they created in their minds to live in had suddenly disappeared, leaving only this horrible mess behind. They had begun to notice the hills and holes in the carpets. They had also begun to notice the many bruises they themselves were always covered with as a result of the falls they were constantly taking in the process of ignoring those hills and holes.

Back in the old days when Coren himself first decided to live in reality, it was the bruises that had most surprised and unsettled him. It had taken him some months of abstaining from the use of his imagination before he was completely healed.

No wonder his mother was so distraught. No wonder she was having such a hard time paying attention to the entreaties of Lenora's parents.

But she did, after Coren made her sit and actually listen to them.

"Oh, Savet dear," Queen Milda said, "I'm so sorry! I got so caught up in my own problems that I almost totally forgot about the wedding! It's hard to think straight, you know, when it's only mere thoughts!"

"Never mind, dear," said Savet. "I should have been paying more attention. I had no idea! What's a little bit of dust when the Balance is being threatened?"

"What indeed," Kaylor said acidly. Everyone pretended they hadn't heard.

"What I think," Arno said, emitting a cloud of flour as he arose from the chair his wife had forced him down into after she dragged him out of the kitchen against his will, "is that you'll all feel better with full stomachs. Let me go and get some of the sugar cookies I just made—still warm from the oven."

"Real cookies," Kaylor snapped, "from a real oven! I warned you, Arno—I told you not to do it! And now this!"

"But," Arno protested, "we couldn't serve our guests from other lands the food we usually eat, could we? It'd just be horrible blue mush to them! That wouldn't be very polite, would it? Would it, Savet? Rayden?"

Lenora's parents completely agreed but weren't sure

whether it would be polite to admit how disgusting they thought the blue mush was. They smiled uncomfortably.

"And anyway," Arno continued, "real cooking is fun! Reality isn't all bad, Kaylor. You shouldn't knock it if you've never tried it."

Kaylor gave him a look of sheer horror.

"Honestly, Kaylor," Coren said to the Thoughtwatcher, "do you really think Father's cooking could disturb the Balance? It's hard to believe that a few real eggs and raisins could have that effect."

"Anything is possible," said Kaylor darkly. "Anything."

"So," Rayden said to Milda, "all this"—he gestured around the room—"is just as upsetting to you as it is to us?"

"It doesn't look any different to me than it always has," said Coren, who didn't find it upsetting at all. "Home sweet home."

"Yes, dear," Queen Milda said, "that may be. But as you know, the rest of us never noticed any of this awful reality before. Why, as far as I was concerned this room was absolutely perfect. Rainbows everywhere, chairs like fluffy white clouds floating over the mirrored floor and singing in unison. I *loved* those chairs." Tears appeared in the corners of her eyes.

"That was nothing," King Arno said, so caught up in his enthusiasm that he didn't even notice the tears. "For me there were deer heads on the walls—deer I'd hunted down all by myself, you know—and big deep chairs to sit in, and a snooker table. Almost as nice as my new kitchen!"

Lenora glanced at the chairs they were talking about. Some of them had lost their coverings and the stuffing was leaking out. Some had springs sticking out, and a few of them even had broken legs. The Andillans did have good imaginations, she had to admit that. And no wonder they were all so black and blue and covered in scratches, if the chairs they actually sat in while they imagined wonders were so damaged and rickety and dangerous.

"Is everyone in the castle affected?" Lenora asked.

"Everyone," Kaylor replied.

"Not Bribden," said Arno, "and not Slidgo. Not as far as we know, at least."

"Who is Bribden?" asked Milda.

"Yes—and who is Slidgo?" asked Kaylor.

"Come now," said Arno, "you know perfectly well who they are. They're my closest advisors, of course. Why, it was Bribden who first suggested the marriage between Coren and the Gepethian princess—Lenora here. For some reason, I haven't seen him lately, or Slidgo either. Had to leave the court for some reason or other, I suppose. But as far as we know, at least, their powers haven't been affected."

"But, Arno dear," said Milda, perplexed. "Slidgo? Bribden? I've never heard of either of them."

"Humph," said Kaylor. "Of course you haven't heard of them. They don't exist—never have. They're obviously advisors that Arno imagined."

"Nonsense," Arno objected. "Why, I've been listening to the advice of those two ever since I was just a boy. It was Slidgo who insisted on stainless steel for the stoves and sinks in my new kitchen. I couldn't run the country without the two of them."

"You made them up," Kaylor insisted. "Why else would they have suddenly disappeared, at the very moment when we all lost our powers?"

"But . . . but . . . I made them up? My old friend Slidgo? Trusty Bribden? They seemed so real. Their advice was so wise, so sound. Oh, dear." Arno sank back down into his chair, clouds of flour mixing with clouds of dust. Milda sneezed.

Deer heads on the wall were one thing, Coren thought.

Imagining people into existence in your mind without even realizing they weren't actually real was another matter all together.

And Arno depended on those figments to guide his every move, apparently. Now that he knew they weren't real—who was going to run the country?

"What about outside the castle?" Coren asked. "Do people out there still have their powers?"

King Arno and Queen Milda glanced toward each other, looking slightly uncomfortable.

"I guess—"

"That is—"

"Well, Coren," Arno finally said, "we don't exactly know."

"But, Father," Coren said, astonished, "you *should* know. You're the king, aren't you?"

"I suppose so," Arno said. "I mean, yes, of course. But good heavens, Coren, put yourself in my place. I don't know what to do—how to get in touch with them, I mean. I've always communicated with my subjects mind to mind."

"Of course he has," said Kaylor angrily. "As he should have. Direct communication is against the laws of nature, if I do say so myself—and heaven knows I ought not to be doing it. Out of mind, out of sight—that's my motto."

"Now wait a minute," King Rayden said. "Let me get this straight. You've never actually been in contact with any of your citizens except mentally?"

"Of course not," said Milda proudly. "Why bother? Some of my best friends are just plain ordinary citizens—no royal blood at all, just regular Andillan folks—and they live out there in the country, I believe. Many's the stimulating conversations we've had, too. But I pride myself on the fact that I've never actually been to the countryside—outside of what I saw on our trip to Gepeth, and of course I didn't pay any attention to that."

"That goes for me, too," said Arno.

"And me," added Kaylor.

"So you can't expect us to know what's going on out there—not if we can't use our powers," said Milda.

"Good heavens," Rayden said. "Why don't you just get on your horse, ride out to the countryside, and visit your subjects!"

"I don't *have* a horse," King Arno said despairingly. "Why would I need one? Why would I want one? Don't you remember, when we came to visit you in Gepeth *you* brought us *your* horses."

"Horses are so big," Milda said. "And they need hay and a stable and who knows what else!"

"A horse!" said Kaylor. "What a primitive idea."

King Rayden threw his hands up in disgust.

"*We* have horses, though," Lenora said. "Don't we, Coren?"

"Yes," Coren said, "of course we do! We'll be happy to lend you our horses, Father."

"Nonsense," Lenora quickly interrupted, glaring at Coren. "Our horses are *very* difficult to handle. Especially for someone who's never ridden before. And as for your horses, Father— well, they're used to pulling carriages, not being ridden. No, Coren and I will have to go out into the countryside and see what's what! We'll leave immediately! Come, Coren." She rose to her feet and began to stride out of the room.

"Lenora," he said, "wait!"

"Yes, Lenora," Savet said. "Come back here immediately."

"Please do, Lenora dear," said Milda. "Things are happening much too quickly. I don't even understand *why* anyone needs to go off into the countryside."

"Nor me," Arno said.

Nor me, Coren told himself. How had a trip into the country suddenly become so urgent?

"But don't you see," Lenora said. "It's obvious. Something has disrupted the powers of you Andillans. And there's nothing to explain it here in the palace, is there? Nothing strange or new?"

"Just Arno's sudden interest in baking," Milda said.

"Nonsense," Arno said. "Baking never hurt a fly. Not good baking, that is. Not if you use plenty of baking powder, right, Savet?"

Savet gave him a withering look and said nothing.

"Of course," Arno continued, "there's all you people from Ge . . . uh, I mean . . . uh—" He suddenly turned bright red and looked sheepish.

"The princess is right, Arno," said Kaylor, quickly filling the embarrassing silence. "A little reconnaissance trip is an excellent idea."

"Just what I thought," Lenora chimed in quickly. What she really thought was merely that this was another chance for an interesting adventure, and she wasn't about to miss out on it. Once out of the castle and away from all these interfering parents, anything could happen. She *really* wanted to go—so much it even surprised herself.

"But, Lenora," Coren began. "We can't." He had to stop her, find some way to keep her there—not to mention himself. Once they went out, away from the safety of the castle, anything could happen. He *really* didn't want to go.

Lenora ignored him. "Meanwhile," she said, quickly changing the subject, "I'm sure that I can create a few little things to make everyone here in the castle a little more comfortable. In fact, I'll do it right now."

And she did. Before anyone could say anything the room

had transformed into a completely different place. The floors were polished wood, which gleamed. The walls were covered in a deep burgundy paper, large soft chairs were everywhere, as were small tables with fragrant bouquets of flowers. Best of all, a large table appeared, covered in food—Lenora's personal favorite fried chicken, different kinds of cheeses and fruits and breads, and lots of cakes. Especially chocolate tortes.

"I'm starving," Lenora exclaimed. "I don't know about the rest of you, but Coren and I haven't eaten since breakfast." She grabbed a lovely china burgundy plate and some gleaming silver and began to dig in.

CHAPTER 4

"Lenora!" Everyone said at once.

"You can't!"

"The Balance!"

"It's too dangerous!"

"Do you want me to make it go away?" she asked innocently, waving a chicken leg in the air.

"No!" Queen Milda exclaimed, suddenly rushing over and grabbing a bunch of grapes. "I've had nothing but mush that tastes like mush for days now. Who can eat the stuff? It's revolting!"

"I did offer you some of my special dark pumpernickel, Milda," said Arno, also going over and checking out the table. "And you really didn't need to make all this bread, Lenora. There's plenty in the kitchen." He grabbed a bun and took a large bite out of it. "Hmmm," he said, "not bad, Lenora—for an amateur. Could use a little more baking powder, perhaps."

By this time, Queen Savet was standing by the table also, trembling with rage. "Horrible," she said, staring at all the food. "Get rid of it this instant, Lenora!"

"But mother, I—"

"No buts, Lenora. You know you can't use your powers for individual gain. We've told you that, over and over!"

"But—didn't I just hear something about fixing up some sheets?"

"Sheets," Milda mumbled through a mouthful of grapes. "What sheets?"

"That was different, Lenora, and you know it."

Lenora couldn't see quite how—except that the business of the sheets was kept secret and everyone knew about the food. But it clearly wasn't the time to say so.

Meanwhile, Savet turned to Queen Milda, carefully ignoring the question of the sheets. "I'm sorry, dear, but surely you see that this food has to go—for the Balance, for the health and safety of us all. After all, King Rayden or I could have done this already, but you know we cannot!"

"Hang the Balance!" Queen Milda screamed. "I'm starving!"

The two women stared at each other.

"Now, Milda," King Arno said, quickly swallowing his mouthful of bun. "Savet really is right, you know. We mustn't upset the Balance."

"On the other hand," King Rayden said to Savet as he eyed a particularly tasty-looking apple, "Milda *is* our host. And she hasn't eaten anything worthwhile in days. What do you say, Thoughtwatcher?"

Kaylor had also been hungrily eyeing the food, but she hadn't actually taken any.

"I don't know," she said. "It could be harmful, I suppose—anything can be harmful. And usually is. But, then, on the other hand, what's a little bit of food like this, compared to all of us losing our powers. It surely couldn't make all that much difference. And it's hard to think straight when you're hungry. I don't suppose"—she turned to Lenora— "I don't suppose you could add a few pieces of unbuttered toast and a small glass of hot water—not quite boiling, with a twist of lemon. I have such a delicate stomach these days."

"Of course," said Lenora, and Kaylor held the glass in one hand and the toast in the other.

"Oh, all right," Queen Savet said, not taking her eyes off the fried chicken for a moment, "leave it." King Rayden nodded too. "But," Savet added, "I *insist* you at least wash up before you eat, Lenora."

"There's no water, Mother," Lenora said smiling.

"Then make some!" Savet ordered.

So Lenora put a little gold sink with pure running water in the corner and hurried over to wash. As she scrubbed with lemon-scented soap (her favorite, so why not imagine it?) Coren came up behind her and whispered into her ear. "What is this all about, Lenora? This trip out into the country, I mean?"

"Well," Lenora said over her shoulder, "someone has to go. Why not us?"

Coren could think of about a hundred and fifty reason why it shouldn't be them, most of them having to do with being safe and warm. And just why did anyone have to go at all anyway? It still didn't make any sense.

But this clearly wasn't the time or the place to talk about it.

"Listen, Lenora," he said. "When I lived here, I made myself a room that was quite nice—a real room, not an imaginary one. Did all the carpentry myself, with some old tools I found down in the dungeon. After we eat, lets go see if it's still there, and we'll plan what to do from there."

"Agreed," Lenora said. "Our parents are acting worse than babies, for heaven's sake. We'll need some peace and quiet to think what to do."

As Lenora and Coren were busily stuffing their faces, Agneth entered the room. He was covered in wet sticky mud from top to toe.

"Agneth," said King Rayden. "Where have you been?"

"In a mud puddle, obviously," he said darkly. "A mud puddle which I landed in after two thoughtless young people spurred their horses and rode off without even looking back to see the effects of their actions."

The first effect, apparently, was that Agneth's horse had tried to follow the other two. Agneth's attempts to hold the horse back, the next effect, had made the frightened animal rear, dumping Agneth into the mud. The horse had then headed off after the others. Agneth had been walking ever since.

The Keeper looked absolutely filthy, and absolutely furious— and he didn't yet know what had been happening in the castle, or about Arno's kitchen or Rayden's sheets or Lenora's spread of food. It was, clearly, no time for Lenora and Coren to hang around.

"Oh," said Lenora. "You poor old dear. You must be absolutely famished. Have this." She thrust a piece of fried chicken into Agneth's hand as she strode by him, grabbing Coren with the other hand and saying, "Come, Coren."

Looking over his shoulder as Lenora pulled him through the door, Coren could see the Keeper munching on the chicken. It was going to be exciting when he discovered that he had actually eaten one of Lenora's Balance-disturbing creations. Very exciting. Coren was deeply thankful he wasn't going to be there to see it happen.

CHAPTER 5

Coren's room was still there—a small neat room, in the west wing of the castle. It had a real bed in it with real sheets and blankets, a real lamp, a real carpet, and real drapes on the large window that led out to a small balcony overlooking the court-yard.

It had taken Coren ages to find all these more or less unbroken objects and to drag them from various parts of the castle. It had taken him even longer to sew up the rips in the sheets and blankets and patch the drapes and hang wallpaper on the walls and install new glass in the windows. He'd done it all himself, and in order to do it, he'd had to teach himself sewing and painting and window installing and about fifteen other things from smelly old books in the library. But it had been worth it. It was a real room, a place he could call his own. He had spent many happy hours in it, reading, thinking, dreaming of other ways of living, recording his thoughts and aspirations in his beloved journal.

He'd been missing that journal—it had been foolish of him, he now realized, not to take it with him when he headed off for Gepeth. But now he was back again. He could go over to the drawer in the chest beside the bed and take it out and read it whenever he wanted.

His room—his very own room. He glanced around it proudly—and then, his jaw dropped in dismay.

There was a huge disgusting dragon's head hanging over the

bed. Its malevolent red eyes gleamed, its gooey green scales glistened, its permanently open mouth revealed rows of dangerously sharp teeth blackened from the smoke of its own fiery breath. Where had *that* come from?

As he walked farther into the room, Coren realized that the dragon was not the only new addition to his sanctuary. There was a jumble of unfamiliar objects on the bed—dresses and skirts and hats and other more intimate items of feminine apparel, all mixed together with gleaming metal breastplates and helmets and maces and daggers.

"I told you, Cori," said Lenora's voice. "I told you this blue wouldn't match." The voice seemed to be coming from the little balcony outside the window. How was that possible? Lenora was standing right there beside him, staring up at the dragon.

Except that now she came through the window and walked into the room, wearing a blue hat and unceremoniously dumping a frilly blue skirt onto the bed.

And Coren himself followed behind her.

He and Lenora were standing there at the door watching themselves walk into the room through the window. It was like looking into a mirror—except the mirror had somehow fancied up Lenora's hairstyle and clothing and taken off Coren's shirt and given him a pair of barbells, which he was raising over his head again and again even as he walked into the room.

"Oh no," the Lenora standing beside him said. "Not you two! I'd completely forgotten about you!"

Of course. That wasn't Lenora over there, and Coren could see from the size of that fellow's biceps that it certainly wasn't him. It was Leni and Cori.

Coren tried not to think about all the chaos that had resulted only a few short weeks earlier, after Lenora had the bright idea of imagining a double of herself into existence so that she could leave the double behind to fool her parents and then go off exploring Gepeth all by herself. She'd imagined Leni just like herself in appearance, but gave her the sort of character her parents seemed to wish Lenora had. No gumption at all. All she cared about was clothes.

As for Cori, well, Coren didn't even like to remember how Lenora had fantasized about how much easier it'd be for her to love him if he had more gumption, and accidentally brought Cori into existence. It'd taken Coren some time, and a lot of grief, before he realized that Lenora didn't actually prefer that obnoxious, muscle-bound, brainless hulk to himself. It had taken Lenora herself almost no time at all, thank goodness.

By the time Cori had rushed off to Andilla to slay the dragon that was bothering Queen Milda and King Arno, he and Leni had fallen in love, and she'd followed on after him. They were still in love, apparently—because here they were, the two of them together, in Coren's own private sanctuary.

And that revolting mess on the wall must be the remnants of the dragon. Trust that blowhard Cori to want to hang a disgusting thing like that over his bed.

My bed, I mean, Coren reminded himself.

"What are *you* doing here?" he said to Cori. "This is *my* room."

"Nonsense," Cori said, still raising and lowering the barbells over his head and becoming increasingly breathless, "it's . . . uh . . . my room. I'm the one . . . uh . . . that gathered all this stuff and brought it . . . uh . . . here. It's mine."

Coren had to admit that Cori had a point, sort of. Cori shared all of Coren's memories up to the moment that Lenora had imagined him into existence. As far as Cori knew he *had* brought everything here.

"Yes," said Leni. "Wasn't it ever so clever of him? My Cori

is such a clever sweetums! The best thing is, there's actually a mirror here—a real mirror, the only one in this whole awful castle!" She pranced over to the wall behind the door, where a full-length mirror hung, and then posed and smiled at herself.

Ah, yes, the mirror. As much as Coren hated his goofy freckles and blindingly red hair and everything else about the way he looked, he hadn't been able to resist hauling that ridiculously heavy mirror all the way up three flights of stairs, just so he could spend long hours staring into it and feeling sorry for himself.

"Anyway," Cori said to Coren, "I might ask the same thing myself. What are *you* doing here, oh he-of-few muscles?" With one final deep sigh, he dropped the barbells to the floor, then strode over to the mirror, pushed Leni out of the way, and began flexing his biceps. "Not bad," he said to his image. "Not bad at all. A truly knightly physique." Still flexing, he looked over his shoulder at Coren with a sneer on his face.

He was right. After just a few weeks of having Cori control it, the body that had started out being exactly the same weak, skinny mess as his own looked completely different. I wonder how heavy those things are, Coren thought, looking down at the barbells. I wonder if *I* could—

"You know full well what we're doing here," Lenora said, watching with distaste as Leni and Cori jockeyed for position in front of the mirror. "We're the ones that are getting married, remember?"

Leni took one look at Lenora and sniffed. "Well, better you than me! I wouldn't get married in this pigsty if my life depended on it."

What a lamebrain, Lenora thought. So thoughtless. How could Leni make a comment like that right in front of Cori, who she claimed to love? Cori had Coren's memories, after all—he thought of this so-called pigsty as his home.

"Me either," Cori said, beginning to run on the spot. "What a cowardly fool I used to be—actually refusing to use my powers to imagine this place any better than it is."

"Now, now, Cori darling," Leni scolded. "You shouldn't be too hard on yourself. I mean, it's true this place is disgusting, and it could certainly use a major freshening up. But I think it was wonderful of you to refuse to use your powers. So sane. So balanced."

"I suppose so," said Cori. "Still, I miss them now that they're gone. It hard to believe that I went on a crusade against a whole battalion of evil invaders just last week, and killed each and every one of them all by myself. And now—well, no powers, no battles, no anything. Nothing but blue mush all the time. It's hard to bulk up on blue mush."

"I know, Cori dear," said Leni, "and I hate that awful mush as much as you do. But if you ask me, you're better off without your powers. Why, every time you had one of those silly battles of yours you wouldn't say a single word to me for hours and hours. You'd just sit there and stare off into space and shout terrible foul language at people I couldn't even see. *And* it made you all sweaty and horrible. Anyway," she added, smirking and fluttering her eyelids at him, "you've still got me, haven't you?"

"Yes, dear," said Cori, smiling at her fondly. "I suppose so." Then his gaze returned to his own image in the mirror, and he flexed his biceps again and smiled even more fondly.

Hmph, thought Lenora, the besotted fool is so in love with himself that it's amazing he has time for Leni at all. If he did have his powers, he'd probably be so busy imagining himself saving the day and being praised for it that he'd never get around to paying any attention to Leni whatsoever.

Just a minute, Lenora thought. Leni didn't like Cori using

his powers. And meanwhile, Leni herself had her own powers intact—and since Leni was actually Lenora in almost every way, her mind was as strong as Lenora's. Could Leni possibly be responsible for what was happening in Andilla? Could she have stopped Cori from imagining to keep him interested in her? Could she have stopped them all from imagining better places in their minds because she herself could see only the ugly truth there and couldn't stand the others not having to see it too? Surely she wasn't that totally petty?

Anyway, Lenora reminded herself, the reason Leni had to be content with the ugly truth was that she was a goody-goody and always did what she was told and refused ever to use her powers. So it couldn't be her causing this imbalance. Could it?

"When Cori and I get married," Leni was saying, "it will be at home. In my own wonderful stylish castle, back in Gepeth, with a full orchestra and proper pew ribbons. We've only been hanging around here waiting for *your* silly little wedding. Thank heavens it's finally going to happen and we can get on with the real celebration back in Gepeth."

Lenora began to steam. "May I remind you," she said through clenched teeth, "that it is *my* home you're thinking of. Not yours. Why would Mother and Father put on a wedding for a figment of my imagination?"

"How *dare* you?" Leni yelped. "*You're* the figment, if you ask me. I certainly don't recall you ever existing at all, not until that awful moment when I took it into my head to imagine a double of myself. What *could* I have been thinking of? You've been nothing but trouble ever since I did it. The only good thing about it is that it certainly taught me my lesson—I'm never going to upset the Balance by using my powers without Daddy and Mommy's permission ever again."

Well, obviously the troubles in Andilla weren't Leni's

fault—unless, of course, she was lying to distract Lenora's attention.

And anyway, how dare Leni imagine that she had made up Lenora? Leni was completely and totally infuriating. In fact, Lenora was just *that* far away from imagining Leni out of existence altogether. The only thing that had stopped her so far was concern over extinguishing a human life, and Leni was hardly acting much like a human. Create me, indeed, thought Lenora. Hah!

Of course, Lenora reminded herself, Leni was just like Cori. She had all of Lenora's own memories up to the moment she'd been imagined into existence. As Leni saw it, she *was* the one who did the creating. Lenora herself was just a figment of Leni's imagination.

"Ooh," Lenora said, glaring at Leni. "You are so infuriating!"

"Not half as infuriating as you are," Leni said, glaring right back at her.

For a moment, Coren observed them both. Lenora was so lovely when she was angry—her cheeks blushed lusciously, and her eyes flashed fire. And Leni looked almost the same.

But it was no time for his mind to be wandering. "This isn't getting us anywhere," he said. "Let's try to calm down. Please."

Lenora and Leni turned to him, their eyes still flashing.

"I can fight my own battles, Coren," said Lenora.

"Mind your own business, Mister Busybody," said Leni.

"That's right," said Cori, jogging closer to Coren and giving him a dirty look. "Gentlemen do *not* order ladies around against their will. It isn't knightly, sirrah. Please cease and desist." By now Cori was jogging on the spot right in font of Coren, nearly stepping on Coren's toes while he shadowboxed with his fists almost in Coren's face.

"Now look here, Cori," Coren said, making fists of his own. "This is *my* room. And I don't care how big your stupid muscles are or how fat your stupid head is, you're not going to push me around in my own room. You can just get out of here, right now!"

"Oh, indeed," said Cori. "And who, Sir Ribs-Sticking-Out, is going to make me? How about *you* get out of *my* room!"

Coren and Cori stared at each other with daggers in their eyes.

It was like getting mad at your image in the mirror, Lenora thought as she watched them. Same adorable face and freckles, and now that Coren was finally aroused enough to lose his shy restraint, the same angry look on the face, the same courage, the same intensity. For all their apparent differences Coren and Cori were really not so different after all.

Whereas she and Leni were completely different. Leni was bossy and self-centred and thoughtless, whereas she herself—

Suddenly, Lenora found herself giggling.

"What's so funny?" Coren asked.

"Yes," said Cori. "What?"

"What indeed?" said Leni.

"Never mind," Lenora grinned. "It's a private joke." Well, if they didn't see the humor of it, then she certainly wasn't going to bother to try to explain it to them. One thing, though, was perfectly clear. She and Coren were going to have to get rid of Cori and Leni if they wanted to get any serious thinking done.

"Listen, Cori," Lenora said, "Coren and I want some peace and quiet—and I imagine you both do, too. And this *is* Coren's room, after all. You and Leni are simply going to have to leave, and that's that."

Cori turned his fists in her direction. "I beg to differ, m'lady," he said. "Not that you're acting much like a lady."

"If anyone should leave," sniffed Leni, "it's you. Go find something really funny to laugh at for a change. Like that blouse you're wearing, for instance."

Lenora sighed. "Coren, let me just imagine them away. Not permanently, of course—just somewhere else."

"What?" Leni said in a shocked voice. "Use your powers? For personal gain? You just wait until I tell Daddy!"

"Hmph," said Lenora. "You might be interested to know that 'Daddy'—who is, incidentally, my father, not yours—has already let me use my powers for personal gain. He and Mother and all of the rest of them are downstairs in the throne room at this very minute, enjoying the feast I imagined for them."

"Feast?" Cori stopped jogging and turned toward Lenora. "You mean food?"

"Yes, of course, food. Fried chicken, fruit, rolls—"

"Food!" Cori interrupted. "Real food! Not blue mush! Let me at it! At it, at it, at it!" Cori was already out the door, without even waiting for Leni.

"Cori! You can't go out in public without your shirt on! Oh, honestly!" Leni stamped her foot, then jumbled through the mess on the bed, found Cori's shirt, and rushed out after him.

CHAPTER 6

"Well!" Lenora said. "At least that got rid of them. What *are* we going to do with those two?"

"I don't know," Coren replied. "But if that muscle-bound idiot dares to come back up here to *my* room again, I'll—well, all I can say is, he'll be sorry."

Lenora had an idea. Cori and Leni were duplicates of herself and Coren who thought they were the real thing. What they needed was a duplicate of this place to be in—a separate place that they would believe to be the real thing. That would keep them far away from this room, and from herself and Coren.

Quickly, Lenora imagined a room exactly like the one she was standing in, dragon's head and all. She placed it right next to this one, with a door looking exactly the same—and then, she changed the door of this room to look like just another part of the wall paneling, until you looked close enough to see the button you had to push to make it into a door again. Now, after Cori and Leni had their food and came back up, they'd return to the new room next door, not even realizing it was a different place. She and Coren would be free to be alone and get on with thinking things through.

"Never mind about those two, Coren," she said. "I have a feeling they won't be bothering us for a while. Let's get to work." She cleared a space for herself on the bed by pushing everything there onto the floor and sat down. "As I see it," she said, "the main thing is to figure out why. *Why* has everyone lost their powers?"

"Humph," Coren said, still bristling. "Maybe that muscle-bound oaf used up everyone's energy imagining all those evil invaders for himself to fight."

"Coren, really, that isn't even logical. You told me your mother dreams up dancing trees and singing chairs and things far more complicated than a few silly invaders every single day, and she never used up anyone else's energy."

"I suppose not," he said, sitting down on the bed beside her. "Only he makes me so mad."

"I know how you feel. For a while there I thought Leni might be responsible, until I remembered how much she hates to use her powers."

"Hmm," Coren said, "I never thought of that. Leni could have done it, couldn't she? She has the power, that's for sure. Just like you. Come to think of it . . ."

"Surely, Coren," she said, punching his arm, "you can see that for once it can't possibly be me? I wasn't anywhere near the palace when it happened."

"Ouch," he said. "That hurt. I was only teasing."

"Teasing? You know what that deserves?"

What it deserved was a kiss that lasted long enough to make them both breathless.

"I thought," Coren said as he came up for air, "that we were supposed to be concentrating."

"Huh? Oh yes. Concentrating." Lenora shook her head to clear her thoughts. "Let's consider the possibilities. So far, we've eliminated Leni and Cori."

"If only we could," Coren said grimly. "If only we could."

"I can, of course, blot them out totally. But I won't, because I'm too kind and thoughtful."

"Of course you are," he said, a knowing smile on his face. "As kind and thoughtful as a herd of stampeding elephants. Which means, I guess, we have to eliminate you. Ouch! Stop hitting me. Eliminate you from the list of suspects, I mean."

"Good. Just keep right on meaning it. So who's left?"

"It can't be your parents."

"No. The situation is driving them both crazy. Not to mention the rest of the Gepethians who've come here for the wedding. And none of the other guests have arrived yet. Which means we've eliminated everyone here at the court who might be responsible. Which is why we have to go out into the countryside and see what's happening there."

"I don't know," Coren mused. "Perhaps it's some *thing* in the castle, rather than some one. You know, like a germ or something. I've read about germs in the old books I found down in the library. I believe they really existed in our world before people imagined them away. Some kind of an infection. Perhaps the court has been invaded by a germ that stops people from imagining properly."

Lenora shook her head. "That's a very bizarre theory, Coren. There must be some simpler explanation than that." Actually, she thought it was pretty clever—she remembered germs from some of her own fantasy books and it did seem sort of plausible. But if she agreed to the idea, she'd be deprived of her jaunt out into the countryside. And she *really* wanted that jaunt. How much she wanted it was surprising.

"I suppose," Coren said, "it does seem more likely that it'd have something to do with Gepethian abilities. What else could change reality so drastically? And come to think of it, Lenora, I can remember the occasional time when you caused trouble with your abilities and you didn't even know you were doing it. So it might be you after all—not that I think it is, of course, so keep your fists to yourself. Or it might be your parents, or Leni. Who knows, maybe Agneth is having some sort of subconscious response to all the unbalanced imagining going on here in Andilla—it must really drive him mad. Maybe he's the one. Maybe we can't eliminate any of them after all."

"Maybe not," she admitted grudgingly. "But I still think we should go out of the castle and investigate. It's obvious that the sooner we get out into the countryside and see what's happening, the sooner we'll know how *really* serious things are."

Coren sank down onto the bed. "I suppose you're right," he said. "I hate this."

He really did feel awful. It was bad enough not having his powers—it was almost as bad as the first time he lost them, when he'd suddenly realized he had always used the powers even when he told himself he wouldn't and thought he wasn't. Without the tiny thoughts of various trees and rocks and pieces of furniture there to guide him, he'd had to learn to walk all over again. Now, once more, he was surrounded by that eerie total silence. And if that wasn't bad enough, Lenora wanted to drag him off on yet another harebrained adventure.

Lenora looked at him sympathetically. "Don't worry," she said. "We'll solve this, no matter what it takes."

Coren smiled ruefully. "That's what I'm afraid of."

CHAPTER 7

*T*he gray mist swirls around her although she can feel no wind. It's so thick it's almost like being blind. Blind but not deaf. Because out of the silence she can hear the voice. "Lenora! Lenora! Come to me. We are one."

She tries to scream, but her voice evaporates. She tries to remember who she is, what powers she has, but she can change nothing, do nothing.

She moves toward the voice. It is so compelling.

"I'm coming."

"Lenora, hurry! Lenora!"

"Lenora! Hurry up! Wake up, for heaven's sake!"

Lenora sat up with a jolt.

"What is it?" Coren asked.

"The dream," she said. "I had that dream again. About Hevak. He was calling me, exactly the way he did that horrible time, remember, back in Grag? And I was going to him, Coren. I was actually going. What if you hadn't woken me up? What would've happened if I'd reached him?" She realized she was trembling.

Lenora never trembled. Coren had been asleep on the thick mattress Lenora had imagined for him on the floor beside the bed when he'd been awakened by her cries. Now he sat down beside her on the bed and put his arms around her. For a moment, she clung to him.

He hated to admit it, but he was thrilled. Lenora was always so brave, so fearless. He never felt needed. And now he did.

Until she shook him off and stood up. "That dream was awful!" She shuddered. "And look, Coren, it's daylight already. Let's get moving! Is there a working bathroom somewhere?"

"Through that little door there, beside the dresser—but you'll have to wait a bit for the water. Plumbing is not my main talent."

Well, Coren told himself as he carefully made up the bed, she *had* needed him—even if it was only for about half a minute. Anyway, he knew she relied on him—just not as her protector. And that made sense, sort of, since he relied on *her* to protect *him*.

But why was she dreaming about Hevak again?

If he didn't know better, he'd be tempted to think that maybe it really *was* Hevak, in person, and not a dream at all—and if it was, well, there couldn't be a better explanation for why the Andillans had all lost their powers. After all, it had been Hevak who was responsible the last time Coren lost his powers.

But, of course, it couldn't possibly be Hevak. Coren himself had been there when Hevak had been absolutely and completely demolished, totally blotted out of existence.

"Horrible dream," Lenora said, returning with a wet toothbrush in her hand. "Maybe it's all that fried chicken I ate."

"I wouldn't be surprised," he said. "Or the chocolate torte you almost finished all by yourself."

"When I *do* imagine the perfect world," Lenora said, "I'll be able to eat as much chocolate torte as I want without a single nightmare."

It took the two of them only a few short minutes to finish dressing and sneak down the stairs and out to the stables. After Lenora had seen the furious look on Agneth's face last night when she had gone down to clear up the remains of the feast, she had decided that they'd better just go without letting the others know about it. It was obvious that if anyone down there knew that they planned to go they'd be stopped for sure.

As their horses trotted away from the palace, Lenora turned to Coren. "You know," she said, "something just occurred to me."

"What?"

"You haven't told me you don't want to go on this trip—not once all morning. You never want to go with me when I have what *I* consider to be a perfectly sensible plan. Why are you coming now, when I—"

"*Don't* have a sensible plan?" he interrupted, giving her a strange smile.

"No, of course not, that's not what I mean, It's just—oh, no you don't! Don't try to change the subject. What I want to know is, why aren't you whining?"

Coren shook his head at her. "Really, Lenora, it *is* my country. I *am* the prince and I do have my responsibilities. Of course I have to find out what's wrong. Even," he added in a smaller voice, "if I don't really want to."

She smiled. "Good for you, Coren."

"And even," he added, smiling again, "if the plan isn't sensible."

It was the only plan they had, though, wasn't it? To Lenora, it seemed the right thing to do somehow, coming out here into the countryside.

She looked around, searching for clues as to why that might be true. They were traveling on a narrow dirt road overgrown with grass and spotted dangerously with mud-filled holes. The fields around them were covered in weeds and wild grasses, with an occasional crop of blue-topped something. The few signs of human occupation they'd seen were the wrecks of old houses, tumbled down and roofless, and the occasional piece of unrecognizable machinery rusting into the ground.

"You know," she said, "I don't mean it as an insult or anything. But your country is really horribly ugly."

"That's because no one takes care of it," Coren agreed. "A result of living solely in your imagination."

"What is that blue stuff?" Lenora asked, pointing to the fields.

"I have no idea," Coren replied. "I've never actually been this far away from the castle before—except for traveling to Gepeth, of course, and then my mind was too occupied with other, well, things, to notice much of anything."

"Could it be what your mush is made from?" Lenora persisted. "It must be made from *something*—and it's exactly the same awful color."

"I suppose it could be."

"But who grows it, then? And how does it get turned into mush?"

Coren felt quite embarrassed. "You know," he admitted, "I have no idea. The mush is just always *there*, you know, in the big vats outside the courtyard—you just go get some when you need some or have your servants bring it to you. And no matter how low the vats get by night, they're always full again every morning. I have no idea about how it gets there at all. Magic, maybe?"

"Good heavens, Coren," Lenora said. "I'm surprised at you—not knowing an important thing like where your food comes from. Haven't you ever been curious about it?"

"No," he said. "I haven't, in fact. But I am now that you've brought it up."

"Interesting," Lenora mused. "Perhaps you've had some sort

of mental block—perhaps it's something you Andillans are not supposed to think about?"

"I don't know. I've never thought about it."

"Which means it could be a clue. What did they teach you about the mush in school?"

"Nothing, of course. We just studied one thing all the time—how to use our minds to their fullest."

"Well, if you ask me," Lenora sniffed, "you're not using your minds all that fully if you don't even know where your food comes from."

"That is exactly the sort of thing I used to say all the time—which is why I got kicked out of school."

"And yet even you never wondered about the food. Interesting. Very interesting."

CHAPTER 8

They traveled through the bleak landscape for two or three more hours before they reached the first hamlet. It looked to be in the same shape as the castle. The small cottages were literally falling apart, as if repairs hadn't been done in hundreds of years, and the ruts in the street were so deep that their horses stumbled and nearly lamed themselves again and again.

There were, however, people here—the first people they'd seen since they'd left the castle. They were clothed in tatters, and the tatters hung loosely on their emaciated bodies. Most of them had monstrous nests of uncombed and unwashed hair that hid most of their unwashed faces, and the men had unkempt beards stained the lurid blue color of Andillan mush. They stood at various points in the village, some inside what was left of the houses and some in the ruts of the road, all wailing and whining and paying no attention at all to each other.

"Hail," Lenora shouted as she pulled her horse to a stop in the center of the village. "Greetings!"

But nobody paid any attention.

"Helloooo!" Lenora shouted. "Is anybody there?"

They all just kept right on wailing.

Lenora was getting annoyed. She imagined her voice to be as loud as a choir of two hundred. "PRINCE COREN HAS ARRIVED!" she shouted. Her voice broke the one window in the village that had still been intact.

But it got the villagers' attention. "The prince?" a woman said, looking up at Coren and moving toward him.

"The young prince who thinks he's too good for us?" added another woman, also moving closer. "The young prince who went off to marry some handicapped princess from Gepeth?"

"She's mad, I hear," another said. "Not to mention her disability. Serves him right, if you ask me."

Soon everyone in the village had gathered in a circle around Coren's horse, all staring up at him distastefully.

"Some prince," a man said. "Just look at those awful freckles!"

"And that hair!" someone else added. "It looks like a bunch of roosters sitting on his head."

"This here is the prince who refuses to use his powers? You'd think someone with hair like *that* would want to imagine himself looking different even more than the rest of us!"

"How true!"

By now, Coren was blushing so brightly that his freckles had disappeared into the general redness. Lenora was furious.

"How dare you," she said. "Making fun of another person's appearance. Have you had a good look at yourselves lately?"

The villagers turned and began looking at each other, and then down at their own rag-covered and filth-stained bodies.

"Oh!" a woman said.

"I forgot!" a man added.

"Mommy!" a child wailed.

The crowd began to wail again, completely forgetting about their guests.

"HOLD IT!" Lenora shrieked, her voice huge again. There was a sudden silence. "I want you all to apologize to your prince," she said.

For a moment they just stared at her, sulking.

"NOW!" she demanded.

They cast their eyes down toward the ground. "We're sorry, your majesty," a couple of them mumbled.

"I should hope so," Lenora said, her voice returning to normal. "And now I want somebody to tell me what you're all moaning about."

"We've lost our powers," an old man said in a halting voice.

"In all my days," a woman added, "I've never thought to see such misery! Look at this place. It's a putrid swamp of decay, a moldy morass of muck!"

Lenora tried not to giggle. She hadn't lost the power of description.

"And my voice hurts," another woman croaked. "Who ever heard of having to speak aloud all the time? It's so noisy. Such a primitive way to communicate."

"Has everyone here lost their powers?" Lenora asked.

"Everyone," the old man answered.

"Even the babies are beginning to make disgusting gooing sounds," a young woman added. "It's quite revolting."

"And look how thin we are," another man added. "No one can swallow that mush. It's vile!"

Lenora and Coren had heard enough. This problem was obviously not confined to the castle. But was it everywhere in Andilla? They had to travel on.

"You are not alone," Coren told the people, trying to reassure them. "Everyone back at the castle has lost their powers too. Including me."

"That's terrible," the old man said. "The castle, too!"

"The king and queen deprived of their powers!"

"It's a disaster!" one of the women added. And soon they were all wailing yet again.

Coren had been planning to give them a few princely words of encouragement, but it was obvious they were not going to listen. He gestured to Lenora, and they kicked their horses to a trot, quickly moving out of the hamlet.

Meanwhile, Lenora had been thinking—as well as she could think with all that mindless caterwauling going on. "You know, Coren," she said once they were back on the road, "something is very odd. I mean, there seems to be a flaw in the system."

"A flaw? The system?"

"Yes. Think about it. Everyone losing their powers like this, well, it's bad in itself, of course—but it also shows you that something was very wrong in the first place anyway."

"I don't get it."

She sighed impatiently. "If this hadn't happened, Coren, you Andillans would have gone right on imagining everything was fine, totally ignoring actual reality. Your houses and streets and clothes and everything would have gone right on getting worse and worse without any of you ever realizing it. I mean, look at what a state things are in!" She pointed to the building they were passing. It appeared as if it might once have been an inn by the side of the road, but now it was just the skeleton of a building, a roof and floors but no walls. As they passed by, huge flocks of birds, the only inhabitants, rose out of it, screeched at them, and then settled again.

"Yes," Coren agreed, "I suppose you're right. I remember when I was little, I used to play in the large banquet hall back at home. But then the roof started to leak, and one day I went in there and the floor had rotted from the wet and fallen through to the cellar. And it's still like that—no one's ever bothered to fix it. After a few people took some serious tumbles and broke a few limbs, the word got out, and everyone simply stopped using that room."

"It hasn't stopped them from falling in other damaged

places or bumping into other broken things, though, has it? And what about the dirt? Don't any of you Andillans make *any* provisions to at least keep what is left of your houses clean?"

"None that I know of. I've never heard anyone even talk about cleanliness—except me, and they all think I'm crazy. You're right, it doesn't make sense. Everyone and everything's in bad shape already—and eventually, there'd be nothing at all left. We'd be living out in the open air freezing, with no shelter at all."

"You know, Coren, much as I hate to say it, your country is almost making my country look good! Now *that's* a scary thought."

Soon they reached another village, this one in even worse shape. The people seemed to have completely forgotten how to use their ability to talk aloud. Since they couldn't communicate mind to mind, they were reduced to croaks, grunts, and lots of inexplicable sign language. As soon as they saw the two horses, they rushed over and grabbed onto the reins and the horses' manes and tails and even Coren and Lenora's legs and boots, staring up at them with imploring looks on their faces and grunting incomprehensibly.

"Coren," Lenora said, looking down at the circle of anguished croaking faces, "this is *awful*. We have to help these poor people."

"How?" he asked, trying to shake people off his legs without actually kicking or hurting them.

"Well," she said, "I still have my powers. I could imagine that *they* have *their* powers. At least for a few minutes. So they can talk to each other and maybe comfort each other a little. And get off my legs!"

"Okay," said Coren, "Not a bad idea—I'm about to lose my left boot. But look—include me while you're at it. Not that I need to be comforted or anything, of course. But if I had my powers back, I'd know what they were thinking and maybe learn something about what happened."

So Lenora closed her eyes and imagined that the entire village had their powers back. Everything became absolutely quiet as the townsfolk were finally able to communicate again. They let go of the horses and their riders and stood silently and stared off into space. So did Coren.

Finally, Lenora could stand it no longer. "What is it," she said. "What are you all thinking?"

Coren turned to Lenora. "They want you to keep it like this," he said. "They're so happy to have their powers back. And," he added, a blissful smile on his face, "so am I."

"If it were that easy," Lenora answered with a sigh, "I could've done it for the entire country. But you'll have to tell them, Coren, that even *I* am not that powerful."

In fact, even as she spoke, Coren suddenly stopped being conscious of the luscious smell of tasty hay passing though the mind of the horse beneath him and became so disoriented that he nearly slipped out of the saddle. By the time he'd righted himself, the townsfolk had lost their powers again also, and had gone back to wild gesturing and grunting.

"You see," she said, "I had to concentrate very hard to imagine that for all these different people—too hard to make it last. In fact, I feel a little light-headed—almost weak."

"Weak?" Coren repeated. He was sure he had never heard that word come out of Lenora's mouth before. He hoped the imbalance wasn't spreading. What if she lost her powers, too?

Lenora was thinking out loud, already forgetting about her unusual symptom. "Of course," she mused, "if every Gepethian came together and if we all imagined it at the same time, I suppose we *might* have enough power to give you your powers back."

"Well, then," Coren said, his eyes lighting up, "why not—?"

"'Might,' I said, Coren. We *might* have enough power—and we might not. And anyway, we still wouldn't know what caused this in the first place. It could happen all over again."

"You're right," he sighed. "And that means we'd better be on our way. We're still no closer to finding out what's made this happen."

But the townsfolk didn't want Lenora to leave. They were still there, grabbing at the horse and gesturing to her to give them their powers back, getting more frantic with every passing moment.

"I'm sorry," she shouted out, "I would if I could!" And she and Coren spurred their horses, practically running down some of the villagers who insisted on standing in their way.

Tired and hungry, Coren and Lenora sat wearily on their horses as they trotted down the narrow dirt road.

"I suppose we may as well return to the castle," Lenora said. "This is getting us nowhere, absolutely no—What's *that?*"

"What?"

"*That!*" She pointed off down the road in the direction they were traveling.

Coren looked, then his eyes opened wide and he suddenly stopped his horse. "I have no idea," he said as he continued to stare down the road. "No idea at all."

CHAPTER 9

"Let's get a closer look," Lenora said, and she spurred her horse into a gallop.

"Wait, Lenora," Coren called. "It could be dangerous."

Naturally, she paid him no attention at all and was soon well ahead of him.

"Oh, honestly," Coren muttered. Why even *try* to get her to be sensible? He spurred his horse and followed Lenora down the road toward the strange sight in front of them as fast as he could go.

Lenora was bursting with curiosity. Ahead were green fields, perfectly tilled, and beyond them fruit orchards displaying a mass of pink and yellow blossoms. As she headed toward them, the road under her feet suddenly changed from dirt and potholes to a smooth black surface wide enough for four horses. She slowed her horse and looked around in wonder as she trotted past the fragrant orchard. It was as if she had passed an invisible border.

Now, on her left, a house appeared. Blinding white-painted wood with green trim, large windows, none broken, so clean the glass sparkled in the sunlight. All around the house was a carefully trimmed and perfectly green lawn—she couldn't see a single weed in it. Everything shone as if newly painted or newly grown. Even the sky seemed to be a brighter blue.

It all looked completely normal—which was, of course, completely impossible. Lenora pulled her horse to a stop in front of the house, so that Coren could catch up to her.

"What is it?" she asked as he pulled up beside her. "What's happening here?"

"I have no idea!" he said, panting. He was shocked to see something like this in his homeland.

"Well," she said, "let's find out." She kicked her horse and trotted up the side path to the farmhouse, Coren right behind her. Once up at the front door she leaped off her horse and ran up to the veranda. She knocked on the front door. All was silent. She knocked again. Nothing. She looked at Coren and shrugged. There didn't seem to be any people around—but there had to be people, to keep everything so tidy and clean and organized.

Well, the people must be somewhere, and she had no doubt that the road would lead them to where that was. She got back on her horse and, gesturing to Coren to follow her, headed back to the main road once more. Coren followed, not without a few anxious looks over his shoulder to see if anybody had finally appeared at the farmhouse door. Someone with a weapon, perhaps, a bow and arrow or a sharp lance? Or someone who thought they were trespassing or something and might yell at them. He urged his horse to keep up with Lenora.

As their horses trotted down the wide, perfectly straight road, the two of them kept a sharp lookout for the people who lived here. There were more buildings, and closer together; they seemed to be approaching a town. They slowed their horses to a walk as the road narrowed into a street. Around them were immaculate white houses, all clean, all tidy, all the same size as each other and all spaced the same distance from each other. And each one was surrounded by a perfectly trimmed and exceedingly green lawn.

A shiver ran down Coren's spine. There was something

about this town, these houses. They didn't seem so ordinary after all—they were *too* clean, *too* tidy, *too* perfect. They were all *too* much like each other. And what was something like this doing in the middle of good old dilapidated Andilla in the first place?

Bong! It was a loud bell—Coren could see it hanging up at the top of the high white-painted tower that occupied the exact center of the square they had now entered. *Bong! Bong! Bong!*

As the last bong sounded, the green-painted doors planted firmly in the exact center of the front of each of the white-painted houses that surrounded the square opened, all at the same time. And, all at the same time, people walked through the doors, shut them, and headed off down their cleanly swept sidewalks and past their immaculate green lawns onto the square.

There were men, women, children—people of all ages. Yet they were all dressed exactly the same: long-sleeved dark blue shirts buttoned up to the neck, straight blue pants, blue shoes, blue hats with wide brims. Some carried baskets or boxes, some wheeled carts that had been parked beside their front doors. Some had climbed onto horses, while others rode on small wheeled machines.

The streets were suddenly so full of people walking with such purpose that Lenora and Coren could do nothing but sit there on their horses in the center of it all, immobilized, doing their best to keep the horses from bolting. All of the people seemed to be following a predetermined path, and none of the paths ever interfered with the others, even though all the people were moving through the same space. Watching it was like being in the middle of the works of a gigantic clock as the wheels meshed and unmeshed silently in perfect precision.

Yes, Coren thought as he watched the intricate choreography going on all around him, definitely not ordinary.

The blue-clad figures were so busy moving down their predetermined paths that they didn't even seem to *see* Coren and Lenora. People passed within inches on all sides of them, sometimes so close that for all their efforts, Coren and Lenora could hardly control the horses. But no one actually touched them.

Then Lenora noticed a short person—possibly a boy, but it was hard to tell because they all wore the same clothes. This short person was carrying a large box he could hardly see over. He had just made a sharp turn to his right, precisely in time to avoid being run into by a large man with a pack full of papers on his back who was riding on one of the wheeled vehicles. And now, the boy was heading right toward the front of Lenora's horse.

Lenora could see that the short person was staring straight ahead of himself—he should have been noticing the horse and doing something about it. But it was obvious he wasn't, because he just kept moving forward at the same maddeningly regular pace. Any instant now he was going to walk right into the horse.

"Hey," Lenora shouted. "You with the box! Watch where you're going!"

Her advice went unheeded. The short person kept right on walking. Soon the box he was holding was plastered right up against the front of the horse. The horse's head draped over it and stared straight down into the person's eyes.

And even then the person still kept gazing straight ahead, though there was nothing to see there but horse—horse so close up his teeth gleamed just in front of the person's glazed eyes as Lenora pulled on the bit with all her strength. Not only that, but the person's feet were still moving, as if he were walking on the spot.

It's a boy, Lenora thought, a boy of around twelve or thirteen. His blue top and pants didn't have a wrinkle in them or a spot of dirt on them—you could still see the knife-edged creases where they'd been ironed. A large round blue hat covered whatever hair he might have, and below it, Lenora could see his pale, almost white skin. His glazed eyes were an equally pale blue.

He still doesn't seem to know that I'm here, Lenora mused. Or the horse.

Well, there was only one thing to do—the one thing that everybody in Andilla seemed to respond to.

"HEY!" she yelled, making her voice the size of a smallish choir.

It worked. The boy blinked. Then his eyes widened and his feet stopped moving.

"What's happening?" he asked. "Twelve points. Why are you there in my path? I'll be late! Late, late, late! Twenty points. To be late, late, late, is an ugly fate! Twenty-five points. Get out! Get out of my path!"

"No," Lenora said calmly. "I won't."

Panic grew in the boy's eyes, and Lenora could see his feet had begun to move again—but, since he hadn't changed direction, they were still not taking him anywhere.

"You have to," he whined. "Forty points. You just have to move! I have to deliver consignment X24A to Warehouse B before the post-meridian cycle is complete! Forty-seven points. I just have to!"

"Well," Lenora said. "I will. But only if you tell me where we are."

"Where we are?" He seemed bewildered. "In Sector Apple Singular, of course. Fifty-four points. In subsector 237 North by Northwest of Sector A1 in Town Number One, Andilla

Central." He looked up at her in deep alarm. "How could you not know what sector you're in, or what subsector? That's—that's scary. Sixty-seven points—plus five extra for scaring me."

Town Number One? Apples? Points? Sectors? Lenora was confused. "Coren," she said, "what on earth is he talking about?"

"I don't know, Lenora. None of this makes any sense to me at all. I don't even know how this place could be here at all, right in the middle of Andilla, when I've never even heard of it! But one thing I do know—you'd better let that poor kid go—he's absolutely terrified."

Lenora could see that Coren was right—there were tears in the boy's eyes as he tried desperately to rush forward, muttering something about points all the while. She looked around her. There seemed to be a fairly clear place with nobody in it just to the right, between her and Coren. She pulled on the reins and gingerly moved the horse into it, just far enough to get it out of the boy's path.

As soon as the horse moved the boy was on his way—his feet had never stopped walking, and now they actually moved the rest of him with them. He didn't even say thank you, just plowed forward, still muttering about points.

Unfortunately, however, the time he'd spent stopped by Lenora's horse meant that he was now totally out of sync with all the other blue-clad people. It was only two or three seconds before he walked right into a woman who carried a large basket on top of her head, with enough force to make her lose her balance. Dropping her hands from the basket, she reached out and grabbed at the box the boy was carrying in order to steady herself. The basket fell from her head, and large blue objects went rolling in all directions. Soon people were walking on them, crushing them, and then, sliding in the sticky mess left behind.

Meanwhile, the boy and the woman holding onto him had

caromed off a man riding on one of the wheeled machines. The force was just enough to change his direction and cause him to drive right into the back of one of the carts, which then speeded up enough to wheel directly into two other people and knock them out of their paths and into three or four others, who bumped into others in turn.

Soon people were bumping into each other all over the square. In no time at all, the entire precise dance was over. The square contained nothing but fallen bodies and people hopping on one leg shrieking in pain and other people yelling at each other about getting in their way. And all of them seemed to be shouting about points and numbers. Lenora and Coren sat on their horses in the middle of it all, the only completely undamaged ones in the lot.

Slowly, the hubbub ceased, as people gradually began to notice the strangers in their midst and began pointing them out to each other. Soon, all eyes had turned to stare at Lenora and Coren.

"I might have known," one of the women finally said. "How did *they* get in here? Four points."

"Haven't seen one of *them* in a long time," another woman said. "Four and two bonuses."

"Haven't been any here for years now, thank goodness. Think they're too good for us, thank goodness."

"Oh yes, always too busy with more important things. Important! Hah! Four."

"Hah," a number of others added. "Four, minus twelve percent for unnecessary repetition."

"Well, one thing's for sure. They're bloody awful nuisances."

"You can say that again. Four."

"Nuisances, the lot of them!"

"Yes, indeed! Four minus a half for agreement."

"Well, we'll just have to get rid of these ones," an old man said. "Just the way we always used to. Sixteen for remembering, by the way. You," he said, grabbing the arm of a young woman who happened to be standing beside him, "sweeping assignment!"

"But I can't," she said. "Not me! Not now! Fifteen points! I'm on mixing duty in Sector B7 in exactly three time sequences. I'll be late. Late, late, late! Forty points!"

"Sorry, dear," a woman near her said. "Sweeping is a category 6. Here—take my broom. Sixty points less thirty percent for civic sanctions makes forty-two. Plus five upon return, of course." She handed the younger woman one of the many brooms that stuck out of a round container on wheels that she had been pushing through the square.

"Oh, all right, if I have to," the young woman said, grabbing the broom. "But," she added, looking at Coren and Lenora astride their horses, "they're quite large, these ones. I'll need some help. You—and you." She pointed to the old woman with the brooms and a rather thin man standing beside her, who both sighed, then each took a broom.

The three of them marched over to Lenora and Coren and began pushing the brooms into the back hooves of their horses.

"Shoo," they said. "Shoo, shoo!" The horses, not liking the brooms pushing at them, began to inch forward, and the blue-clad people in front cleared a path for them.

"Works every time," the old man said. "Add a bonus of eighteen points. Just move 'em down toward Sector G5—once you get them down there they tend to find their own way out."

Lenora turned around and watched in disbelief as the people tried to sweep her horse and Coren's out of the square. Finally, she could stand it no longer. "Just what," she said to the youngest of the women, "do you think you are doing?"

The people holding the brooms froze in mid-sweep and looked up at Lenora, a startled expression on their faces. All the other blue-clad people, who had begun to stand up and dust themselves off and gather their possessions, stopped and turned toward Lenora also.

"You—you can see us?" the old man asked.

"Of course I can see you," Lenora answered. "Why wouldn't I be able to see you?"

"Interesting," the old man said as if she weren't even there. "One of them that actually can see us."

"Is it dangerous?" another man asked in an alarmed voice. "Them seeing us, I mean. It seems, well, wrong somehow. I'm feeling pointworthy alarm."

"You're right," a woman chimed in. "I'm feeling it too, and I don't like it. They shouldn't see us. It's unnatural."

"Unnatural indeed! We'll certainly have to charge them for it, of course."

"Of course. But how much?"

"Unnatural acts are on the D scale—category 5a, subsection 735. I say at least two hundred. Each."

"Nonsense. The D scale doesn't apply here—we have to think about them being mounted, for one thing. That's an exception to D, according to subsection 736, horse actions. We have to use the fiscal integrity formula."

"And they don't belong to our sector. That's a deduction of forty-three percent of the total after wastage, isn't it?"

"Yes, but then there are the damaged Grundellions—my whole basket, smashed! That's twenty-two points each!"

"And," the boy who had walked into Lenora's horse added, "they talked to me first. I've never seen one before, and I didn't even know what it was. Don't forget my five extra points for being scared."

By now, all the blue-clad figures were involved in intensely passionate conversations with each other, discussing points and doing complex calculations. They had once more totally forgotten about Lenora and Coren.

Here we go again, thought Lenora. "HEY!" she shrieked yet once more.

Total silence.

"That's much better," she said. She leaped off her horse and grabbed the closest person to her by the shoulders. It happened to be the boy who'd walked into the horse. "Now," she said to him, "Listen up. I'm talking to you. Pay attention. Just answer one question and then I'll let you go. Okay?"

"Okay," he said in a tiny frightened voice. "But I'm adding five more for illegal holding. And don't wrinkle my shirt."

"Unsought wrinkles are on the X scale," a nearby woman said helpfully. "Double points."

"Good," Lenora said. "Double points it is then—whatever that means. Now, what we want to know is, where are we, and who are you?"

"I told you!" the boy replied angrily. "I told you already! Subsector 237 North by Northwest of Sector Apple Singular, Town Number One, Andilla Central. That's thirteen more for wasteful repetition! *And* there's a six-point wrinkle on my shoulder, which doubles to twelve. Are you sure you can afford all this?" He stared angrily into Lenora's face.

By now, Coren had left his horse and come over to see if he could help. As usual, Lenora's aggressive tactics weren't getting her much of anywhere.

"But you see," Coren said politely, "we didn't understand it when you told us. Can you explain it to us?"

"This," the boy said through clenched teeth, "is subsector 237 North by Northwest of Sector Apple Singular, Town

Number One, Andilla Central. What's to explain?"

"What indeed," said a man nearby. All the blue-clad people, still watching, murmured their agreement.

"Well," Coren said, "It's like this. I'm—" he hesitated, unsure as to whether or not to let these strange people know who he actually was. But he had to, didn't he? So they could understand why he found their unexpected presence in his country so bewildering?

"Oh, for heaven's sake, Coren," Lenora interrupted impatiently. "This is Prince Coren of Andilla. Your country's prince. And *I* am the Princess Lenora of Gepeth." She waited expectantly for the boy to react. She hated to pull rank, of course, but maybe being in the presence of royalty would actually get these strange people to do what they wanted.

The boy inspected them as if he were inspecting an unusual insect. Lenora could just imagine what he saw. Two rather uncourtly figures, traveling without a retinue or any signs of pomp. Lenora's long straight blond hair was tied back in a knot, she wore a long beige riding skirt and a loose brown top. Coren was dressed in a simple pair of brown pants and a leather jerkin over a white shirt. His red hair fell loosely over his shoulders, and they were both dusty from head to toe, especially their riding boots, which were caked with dust and mud. No, not exactly a regal picture. Still, surely if these people were Andillans they would recognize their prince.

"You?" the boy said. "You're the prince?"

"Some prince," someone else said. "Not even in uniform."

"Well," an old man said, "what could you expect of *them*?"

"True, true," a number of others added.

"Prince or not, it'll be two points for each of those ugly red dots on his face."

"Only two? How about codicil 8—the distressing public

spectacles addendum? I sense distress, let me tell you. I'd make it three each, plus a bonus for every ten."

"Now look," Lenora said, totally enraged, as she stormed over to the old man with fire blazing in her eyes. "I don't know who you people think you are or where you think you are. But Coren is the prince of your country. You owe him some respect. You owe him an apology. Right now!"

Coren, watching silently, groaned inside. Just like Lenora to go crashing into a situation with no diplomacy at all—and all in defense of him and his stupid freckles. It was sweet of her, but it was also very dangerous. Still, he certainly wasn't prepared for what came next.

"An apology, eh?" The old man's eyes narrowed and he gave Lenora a crafty look. "Interesting. How much are you prepared to pay?"

CHAPTER 10

Lenora was flabbergasted. "Pay?" she said. "You expect me to pay for an apology?"

"Well, you don't expect to get an apology for nothing, do you? Good heavens. Apologies are at least 150 points, on a sliding scale with peripheral amortization—150 is just the starting point."

"And," a woman nearby added, "don't forget the extra charges for composition and grammar correction to ensure contractual validity."

"I've had about as much as I can take," Lenora said, her teeth clenched. "I'm not paying you for an apology. In fact, I'm not paying you for anything. You can take all your ridiculous points and sliding scales and addendums and—and build a bonfire out of them, for all I care!"

A gasp emerged, simultaneously, from the mouth of each and every one of the blue-clad figures in the square.

"Out-and-out blasphemy!" a woman cried.

"Sacrilege!" another added.

"Gross infamy!" said a third.

"Oh, dear," the old man said. "All things considered—and considering is itself worth eight more, I'm afraid, in case you didn't know—you really leave us no choice at all." He turned and pointed to some men standing near him. "You," he said, "and you. And"—he pointed to the boy who had walked into Lenora's horse—"you, classification Y12. Sanitation patrol.

Confiscation for the public good is appropriate and recommended."

Without a word, the boy nodded, then walked over to the woman with the round container filled with brooms.

"Public good confiscation," he said. "Which is completely pointless behavior, and don't you forget it." Then he lifted the brooms out, dumped them on the ground, and wheeled the empty container over to where the old man was standing with Lenora and Coren.

"Excellent," the old man said. "Proceed."

The other two blue-clad men he had chosen walked toward Lenora and Coren, grim looks on their faces, bent down in front of them, grabbed them around the knees, lifted them high off the ground, carried them over to the round container, and stuffed them in, both at the same time.

It was a tight squeeze for the two of them. If she hadn't been totally furious about being treated in this outrageous way, Lenora might actually have enjoyed it.

Coren, who simply expected to be treated outrageously whenever he was around Lenora, was scared out of his wits—so scared he hardly even noticed Lenora pressing up against him. Where were they being taken? And why?

"Good," the old man said, watching the two of them squirm inside the container. "Exactly where they belong. Now, to Refuse Holding number 8A, subsector S plus S 7. Follow me."

He began to walk. The men took position on either sides of the container, and the boy began to push it forward, following the old man.

"What are you doing?" Lenora said, trying not to fall over. "Where are you taking us?" She considered using her powers to turn them all into cabbages, but she restrained herself—at least long enough to get some answers. *Then* she'd turn them into cabbages.

"Twenty-two more for illicit questioning," the boy said as he pushed. "Honestly! If I were you, I'd just stop talking altogether."

An excellent idea, Coren thought. Especially when Lenora got them into deeper trouble every time she opened her mouth. Especially when she jabbed her elbow into his stomach every time she tried to turn around to talk to the boy.

Lenora, of course, kept right on turning and right on talking.

"When King Arno hears about all this," she said, "you people are going to be in big trouble. Treating your royal prince like this—when you ought to be preparing some sort of fancy reception for him or something."

"Very amusing," the boy said, his face as unsmiling as ever. "Amusement is a felony. You're *really* going to have to pay for that."

As they wheeled across the square, the bell in the tower began to ring again. BONG! It went. BONG! BONG! BONG!

"Oh, dear," Coren heard someone nearby say, "I almost forgot the time."

"Goodness," another said, "I'm completely off schedule now."

"Honestly, those court people are so thoughtless. We've lost at least ten minutes standing here. Ten points in total!"

"Not to mention all the undelivered consumables."

Now the bells were replaced by loud music, blaring from the tower. If, Coren thought, you could call it music. It was really a repetitive beat with some annoying voice repeating a few lines over and over: "Work it hard, work it up, work it hard, work it up."

Looking back over her own shoulder and Coren's as she was

being wheeled out of the square, Lenora could see all the blue-clad people gathering up their dropped utensils and boxes, depositing them by the edges of the square, and then forming into lines. A young woman and young man had moved to a position in front of them, just by the side of the tower, and they seemed to be leading the throng in a series of grueling movements. They were jumping up and down, squatting, leaping to one side then to the next.

None of them seemed to be enjoying themselves. They looked like they were studying a very boring book or something.

"That doesn't look like much fun," she commented.

"Fun?" the boy sneered. "Whoever heard of doing things for fun? Really."

"Enough interaction with the goods, Y12," the old man said over his shoulder. "Sixteen points. And do hurry. I haven't missed an exercise class since I was four years old. If we do this quickly I can still catch most of it."

Lenora rolled her eyes. "I don't think the world will come to an *end*," she said, "if you miss one exercise class."

"*You* have no sense of proportion, obviously," the man said as he walked briskly ahead of them. "Four."

They had now left the square and were wheeling down a wide and spotlessly clean street. Lenora decided to delay punishing them all so she could find out more about where they were. Small shops flanked them on either side, with store fronts displaying what was to be bought inside, each of them accompanied by signs saying: TEN APPLES, 1 POINT or HATS, 10 POINTS. The apples, displayed in even symmetrical rows, were all perfect, and all the same uniform red. The hats were all exactly the same, and exactly the same as the ones all the people already wore.

Coren, meanwhile, had managed to calm himself down a

little. Lenora could get them out of there anytime she wanted to, he reminded himself. At least he *hoped* Lenora could still use her powers. Probably she was too interested in what was happening to bother—and they didn't seem to be in any real danger. He and Lenora were wedged in so tightly that there wasn't even any room for him to shiver anyway. It was calming, somehow—and actually, come to think of it, rather pleasant. Being close to Lenora was always pleasant—and this was *very* close.

He was positioned in the container so that he was looking straight into the face of the boy who was pushing them. Might as well try to get more information, he decided

"We've told you who we are," he said as politely as he could. "Could we, perhaps know your name? If you don't mind, of course."

"No problem," the boy replied. "As long as you're willing to compensate at the usual level. My name is Mud. Mud Sirth, Y12. Twenty points, that is."

"Mud," Lenora said, once more turning to look at the boy and jabbing Coren. "That's, uh—well, very unusual." She almost had to bite her tongue to stop herself from laughing at the incredibly ugly name.

"I don't see what's so unusual," Mud said, alarm in his eyes. "Mud is a perfectly acceptable name. Quite ordinary. Many people have it. Mud Stirth, Mud Birth, Mud Chirth—I know a lot of people whose name is Mud."

"Of course," Coren said reassuringly, giving her an angry look. "Don't be silly, Lenora." He tired to ignore the jab she gave him. "By the way, Mud," he continued, trying to keep the boy interested in talking, "who are these other people?"

"That's Sud Girth in front, O60," the boy said, "and those two are Fud Nirth and Dud Firth—they're both M20s. That'll be twenty points each. Sixty altogether."

"Of course," Coren said reassuringly. "Twenty, each." Fud. Sud. Dud. Well, it was no wonder Mud thought his name was ordinary.

Coren was just about to ask another question when the old man came to a sudden stop. "Halt," the old man said. "Here we are."

They had wheeled up to a large low building at the end of the street, painted white like all the others but windowless. The old man pulled open a wide swinging door, and then the boy wheeled them through it into a huge room filled with round containers just like the one Coren and Lenora were inside of.

"Now, my courtly friends," the old man said, "let me explain a few things to you."

"Good," Lenora said. "It's about time." I hope it's worth the bumpy ride, she thought. Maybe I should turn them into carrots instead of cabbages—they deserve to have their heads stuck in the ground forever.

"Time indeed," the man agreed. "Why, exercise is more than half over by now. Here's the situation—I won't, for once, charge you for explanatory speech. You two are in big trouble. First off, you're trespassing here. We have very strict rules about who comes in and who goes out—and they don't include people like you."

"But this is Andilla," Coren said. "I'm the prince. You can't—"

"I don't care who you are or who you think you are. You courtier types just think you own the world. Well, let me tell you, Prince, once you used our roads you were in our territory. Edict number X77 codicil 6. That means you owe us three hundred points for the use of our road—and that, I'm afraid, is just the beginning. Disruption of public order, interruption and repetition, trying to be amusing—amusing, of all things!—destruction of valuable consumables. Not to mention we're going to have to put together a special committee to even begin to calculate all the points you've managed to ring up—and the committee's going to cost you extra. It's going to be some mighty sum you two owe, believe me. Possibly a record."

"I told you to stop talking," the boy said. "I warned you."

"Enough, Mud."

"Yes, sir, O60," Mud muttered. "But warnings are worth three. I hope nobody forgets it."

"Anyway," the old man continued, "you owe us, and you owe us big. And you're not getting out of here until you pay. Statute 3456a, subsection 2. Is that clear?"

"But," Lenora said, "we don't have any points."

"Or maybe we do," Coren added. "We don't even know what points are."

"You should have thought of that before you started racking them up. Now it's too late. You pay up or you rot here in Refuse Holding along with the rest of the damaged goods."

Lenora did her best to ignore the insult. "But how do we pay?" she asked. "How can we get points if we're stuck in here?"

"You can't. Don't be ridiculous."

"But that's not right!" Coren declared.

"As I said, you should have thought of that before. Now I'm going off to get my exercise—whatever little bit of it is left to get by this late hour, thanks to you. I already feel my abdominals seizing up. Then I'll gather the committee and begin the calculations. You can expect me back here by time frame 5b, post meridian, with a complete itemized bill. You, Y12"—he turned to Mud—"you are to stay here and see that they don't get into any mischief."

Mud was in a panic. "But I'm on schedule 42 in this time frame! I have consumables to deliver to subsector 5B! I'll be late, late, late!"

"Never mind all that, lad. This is a civic emergency. You'll get fifty bonus points—more if there's trouble."

"Well," Mud said, "all right. I suppose. But someone will have to go to consumable dock 23 and inform Cud Tirth M40 of my absence. And move thirty pounds of consumables to the docking by time frame 5c. And tell my mom where I am."

"Yes, yes, of course. Now, Prince, or whatever fancy-schmancy court thing it is you think you are, I'm putting this Y12 in charge here. He'll be right outside the door—which, incidentally, I am locking. And he will be equipped with a weapon. So if you're thinking about trying anything, well, think again. I'm late, late, late. Farewell."

With that he and Mud strolled through the door and slammed it shut behind them, leaving Lenora and Coren in total darkness.

"I think I'll turn half of them into cabbages, half into carrots, and those two into some kind of insects," Lenora said, her voice grim. "I hope they don't think we'll stand for any of this! But first, I'll imagine us out of this container."

Coren nodded, then waited a moment.

"Well?" he said impatiently.

"I just tried," she said in an anxious voice, "and it didn't work."

Coren shook his head. "I was afraid that this might happen. You strained yourself back in that village—remember, you felt light-headed. You overdid it."

Lenora snorted. "I never overdo anything! It's something else. The imbalance is obviously spreading. We're stuck here—and there's nothing I can do about it."

CHAPTER 11

As they stood there silently in the container in the dark, letting the true misery of their situation sink in, they gradually became conscious of an incredibly bad smell surrounding them.

"What *is* that?" Lenora asked, nearly gagging.

"Smells like some kind of rotting fruit or vegetable," Coren said. "That's probably what all those containers are full of. Didn't the old one say this was a refuse area?"

"Yes, he did. Said we belonged here, too. What an insult! And to people of royal blood! Just who do they think they are?"

"That's exactly what we need to know, Lenora. Ouch!" The "ouch" was in response to a jab Lenora had given him with her knee as she tried to move around in the container.

"Lenora," he said, "we're going to have to get out of this thing, or I'm going to be nothing but bruises."

They tried squirming around—fun, actually, being so close, but if anything, it just squeezed them in more tightly.

They tried jumping up. Nothing happened at all.

They tried pushing on the top rim of the container with their hands. They did manage to lift themselves up a little but not enough to jump out—and as soon as they stopped pushing they slid right back down again, putting a number of rips in their clothing.

Finally, they realized there was only one thing to do. They began to rock the container back and forth, back and forth— so far back and forth, finally, that it fell over, causing Coren to bump the back of his head on the floor and Lenora to bump her face into his.

For Coren, it was like being in the middle of a pain sandwich—he couldn't decide whether it was the front of his head or the back that hurt the most. Not that it really mattered anymore, because by now he had so many bumps and bruises all over his body that he hardly even noticed anything special about these last two additions.

Once they'd tipped the container over, it didn't take them very long at all to squirm their way out—although it did cause a few more bruises and scratches and tears in their clothes. Soon they lay beside each other on the floor in the dark, trying not to smell the incredible stench, nursing their wounds and considering their situation.

"Maybe he didn't really lock it," Coren said hopefully. He groped through the darkness on his hands and knees, banging into a few very smelly containers, found the knob, and tried to turn it. Nothing. He began banging on the door, trying to force it open. Nothing.

"Hey," he heard a voice shout. It was the boy, Mud, who must have been standing just on the other side of the door. "Cut that out! I have a weapon! Twelve points!"

"We're prisoners, all right, " Coren said, crawling around in the dark toward where he thought Lenora ought to be. "And no one will ever be able to find us! I can't communicate with anyone in the castle—and since no one there even knows this place exists, how can they look for us? Ouch!" This "ouch" was caused by him crawling right into Lenora and knocking her over again.

"Ouch," said Lenora. "I'm sore all over. And I'm hungry! And thirsty! And this place stinks to high heaven! And my powers are gone and I can't do anything about any of it."

Coren reached out in the dark for Lenora and gave her a comforting hug.

"Maybe we've found out why we're losing our powers," he said grimly. "These people!" Because surely it had to have something to do with them. They weren't supposed to be here at all. Their presence was bound to affect the Balance somehow.

"If only we knew who they were," Lenora said, "or where they came from. Beside Section 60 million of subsector gibberish with fourteen bonus points, I mean."

"If only I had my powers—I could read that fellow Mud's mind and maybe find out."

"If only," Lenora said sadly. She gave his hand a squeeze.

Suddenly, the hand she was holding stiffened, along with the rest of Coren's body. He shook her off and sat bolt upright.

"*And damaged Grundellions,*" he said in a flow of words so fast she almost couldn't understand them, "*a terrible smell, yes, and yes, broom usage, and then there's four for each sentence times thirty-seven, no, thirty-eight and twelve bonuses for repetitions, yes, and the fifty bonus for guard duty not to mention wrinkle protection and that awful amusement business, oh yes, yes, its bound to be at least 350, yes, which is hardly enough for the wear and tear on my clothing let alone the rescheduling, and she actually did try to be amusing, the one wearing a skirt, yes, imagine that, wearing an illegal garment, yes, and being amusing, yes, what kind of person would do such an awful thing, and, yes, she said my name was unusual, too, hah, what nonsense, I always heard they were bad, evil, awful people but I never suspected that they wou—*"

Coren broke off, just as suddenly as he'd began, and slumped back down against her.

"Coren—what is it? What happened?"

"I—I'm not sure." His voice sounded confused. "I think

maybe you imagined I could read that boy Mud's thoughts and it worked." He suddenly sat up again. "It worked, Lenora! Try the door! Imagine it open! Now!"

She did. Nothing.

"It's not working now," she said.

"Well, it wasn't just me getting *my* powers back," Coren added bleakly, "Because I can't hear a single thought now. Maybe *your* powers are working erratically?"

"You did get to read his mind for a moment or two. Did you learn anything?"

"Maybe I did. Sometimes people are thinking about stuff they know without even realizing it, and if you look under the surface . . . Let me see." Coren directed his thoughts inward and began to explore his memories of the experience he'd just had. "There's lots about points in here—his whole head is filled with points, all the time. It must be awful! No wait, here's something a little different, a sort of subconscious thought about Grundellion duty. He doesn't actually like it, because of the smell, and he's sort of glad he gets to sit out there and guard us instead. But he hasn't actually totally admitted that to himself because its such a shameful thought to not like something you're supposed to do, and he doesn't want anyone ever to know that or else they'll think he's crazy. And—and that's all."

"Are you sure?" Lenora asked.

"Yes, I'm sure," Coren sighed. "I guess we have no choice but to sit here and wait."

Which Coren wasn't looking forward to. If there was one thing Lenora hated doing, it was waiting, unable to *do* anything.

CHAPTER 12

Coren and Lenora sat in the dark for hours, ignored by their captors. Lenora had a plan to escape the minute they heard the door open—they would rush Mud, overpower him, and escape. Except that the door never opened. And it and everything else continued to resist Lenora's attempts to imagine them differently.

Lenora was tired, too—that is, she kept having to fight off an urge to fall asleep. Her head would slump forward, her eyes close, and suddenly she could feel the gray around her. The nightmare, ready to begin the minute she dropped off.

"Coren," she said as she snapped herself out of it, "you have to keep me awake. This stupid Hevak dream seems to be there all the time, waiting to grab me."

Coren was concerned. How could a dream keep recurring like that?

"And I'm starved," Lenora complained.

Good, Coren thought. That'll keep her mind off the dream. "Well," he said, "these containers are filled with consumables—isn't that what they said? They must be edible. Should we try?"

Lenora would try anything. She reached her hand into one of the containers and drew out something squishy and slimy. She passed it to Coren, then reached in and grabbed another for herself, took a bite, gagged, and spit it out.

"That's revolting!" she declared, a shudder running through her.

"Hmm," Coren said as he chewed. "Not bad. Not bad at all." She could actually hear him take another bite.

"Not bad? Are you joking?"

"No—it tastes sort of like blue mush but not quite so, well, bland. I've always liked blue mush."

Sitting in the dark and listening to the slurping sounds Coren made as he ate his fill, Lenora found it very hard to stop herself from just crawling right over to him and adding a few more to his collection of bruises. On the bright side, it *had* awakened her and kept her away from that dream.

Without warning, the door opened a crack.

"Here's some consumables," Mud said. "It'll be seventy-five points each, plus the dishwashing surcharge. And stay back—I have a weapon." Then he pulled the door shut, gone as quickly as he had appeared.

Lenora crawled over to the doorway to find a tray sitting on the floor, containing two plates. Lenora couldn't see the food, but she could tell when she picked it up that it each plate contained a series of perfectly square objects, piled neatly on top of each other. They turned out to have absolutely no taste at all—which was better than the taste of what Coren had eaten. She emptied both plates, and still felt hungry.

For some time after that, they tried screaming for someone to come and talk to them. But no one appeared interested in doing so.

"Honestly!" Lenora said. "How do they expect us to get their blasted points if they keep us in here? Shouldn't we be allowed to send a messenger to your parents or something?"

"I'm sure that will occur to them eventually," Coren said.

"I don't want to wait for *eventually*," Lenora said angrily. "I want some fried chicken. I want a nice hot bath. I want to stop smelling that awful stink. I want out *now*."

"So do I, but—"

"Coren! I just had a thought! Maybe I can't get the door open because the energy of these people surrounding us is affecting my powers. I mean, let's face it, they obviously haven't got much imagination. All they think about is facts and figures."

"That's true," Coren mused. "When I was in that boy's thoughts it was like—well, like he had no imagination at all. Not any."

"That's creepy," Lenora said. She couldn't even begin to imagine it. Strange, really—the one thing she could not imagine was not imagining.

"If all the rest are like him," Coren continued, "then it might build up a sort of negative force—stop you and me from using our imaginative powers just because all these people around us don't even know it's possible to use them."

"That's what I was thinking," Lenora said. "But no matter how unimaginative these people are, surely they can't be stronger than me? They can't possibly be—no one ever is, isn't that so?"

It seemed to be a real question, and, for a brief moment, Coren found himself distressed at Lenora's arrogance. But, he reminded himself, she's not being arrogant, just honest, the way she always was. It was the truth—no one ever was as strong as she was. "No one I ever heard of," he told her.

"And," she continued, "back at the castle people still have their imaginations, right? And *they* still believe that *our* powers will work. Maybe that'll help. It should help if I believe it'll help. And I do. I really do. Don't you?"

Coren nodded and tried desperately to mean it—a hard thing to do when it was so completely illogical, but he did try.

"I'm going to use every bit of strength I have and imagine

us being back there," Lenora continued. "And I want *you* to help, too."

"Me? How?"

"You can send out thoughts of the two of us being there and imagine as hard as you can that people in the castle can actually hear you and share your thoughts. Your powers have been working every once in a while, after all, and who knows, maybe we'll hit it lucky."

"Maybe," Coren said hesitantly. "Okay. I guess."

"Come over here and hold my hand. I may have to be touching you to bring you with me." She actually sounded as if she believed she would be going somewhere.

Coren crawled over to Lenora. By this point, he was ready to try anything, even this particularly lamebrained and illogical scheme—and anyway, holding Lenora's hand was always comforting, especially in emergencies like this.

Lenora grabbed on tightly to his hand and shut her eyes. She imagined them back in Coren's little room in the castle in Andilla, pictured all its details in her mind. Then she tried to make what she imagined real, and she threw herself and Coren out of their jail into the castle.

And suddenly, they were there! There was the bed and the dragon's head on the wall.

And there was Leni, sitting on the bed beside Cori.

"If Lenora *was* here," Leni was saying, "she'd probably want to use her powers for sure! She's so impulsive, poor thing! She'd be creating banquets and pouring hot baths for us without any regard for the Balance at all! "

It had worked! Leni had somehow caught Coren's thoughts of Lenora having her powers and being there in the castle— and it had happened exactly as Leni and Lenora had both imagined it.

Well, not exactly. It wasn't Coren's room they'd come to, not if those two were in it. It was the duplicate room she'd made up for Cori. But that didn't matter. She and Coren were safely back in the castle.

Or were they?

Leni was staring at them, and she was screaming!

"What is it! What is it? Oooh, it's too horrible. Cori, are they ghosts?"

Cori jumped to his feet and drew his sword. "Who are you?" he declared. "I'll slice you in half, you vaporous varlets, if you try to harm my precious Leni!"

"We're Coren and Lenora, of course," said Lenora—but nothing much seemed to come out of her mouth. And perhaps that was because not much of her mouth was there. Lenora looked down. She could see right through herself! It was, well, embarrassing. And Coren was the same—hardly there at all, except he had a sort of disgusting bluish mass floating where his stomach should have been.

"It made a strange noise," said Leni. "I'm frightened, Cori. Go away, you nasty thing! Shoo! Shoo!"

Shoo? She was actually *shooing* them. If Lenora had the ability she would definitely get rid of Leni right there and then. But obviously, her powers were *not* working. Not completely, anyway. She'd managed somehow to get them partially here. But where was the rest of her body? It certainly wasn't anywhere in sight. So she had to conclude that it was still back there in the dark refuse room in that peculiar town. How annoying!

For a moment, she considered giving up and returning them to their bodies. But, no, there had to be some way to make this work. There had to be.

Yes. She and Coren would have to find her father and her

mother. They should be able to imagine the *rest* of them back, shouldn't they?

Except how? They'd have to know what had happened. They'd have to know where Lenora and Coren's bodies were. And Lenora didn't seem to be able to speak, not in any way that made sense to anybody. And she had no hands to write with.

And it was *very* difficult to think with Leni screaming and shrieking and shooing. Coren seemed to be trying to calm Leni down, but he was only making things worse. Every time he went near her she began to scream, and Cori lunged at him with his sword, which went right through Coren's bluish stomach. It was disconcerting to see Coren divided in half like that, but it didn't seem to be doing any damage. He immediately joined right back together again.

There had to be some way to stop Leni from screaming. Leni had the same powers as Lenora, after all. If she could just somehow get her to understand, maybe *she* could—

"What's all the ruckus?" a voice said from behind Lenora. "I like ruckuses!"

Lenora turned to see Sayley standing in the doorway—the little girl she'd met on her trip out into the Gepethian countryside, the last time she'd got into big trouble like this. Lenora liked Sayley. After the trouble was over, finally, Lenora had made sure Sayley was invited to the wedding, and even arranged transportation for her, a royal coach with two fine white horses and a footman—and now, apparently, she'd arrived.

"Sayley!" Lenora tried to cry, but only "Aiee!" came out. Leni screamed even louder, and this time Cori cut Lenora herself in half. It sort of tickled but not very much.

Stepping out of the range of the sword, Lenora thought

about Sayley. Young as she was—she was no more than ten years old—Sayley had powers that almost equaled Lenora's. Also, Sayley *adored* Lenora. It would be far easier to get *her* to help them, Lenora thought, than to talk Leni into actually doing something about something other than her hairstyle for a change, or to involve her parents, who would only get so upset seeing her like this that nothing would be accomplished.

"Are you Lenora?" Sayley said to Leni, staring in bewilderment at her complicated hairdo. "Or"—she turned to the ghostly figure—"are you?"

"I'm Leni," Leni replied. "How you could confuse me with that awful Lenora person whose hair is always unconditioned and dreadfully stringy is totally beyond me. And who or what *that* creature is I have no idea! But it scares me, sort of. A lot, actually." She turned toward Lenora. "Shoo!" she said again. "Shoo!!"

Shoo yourself, Lenora thought. She'd had just about all she could take from that shooing ninny. She ran over to Leni and put her ghostly hands around her throat and began to squeeze.

It had no affect of course, because her hands were almost pure air. In fact, Lenora could feel her two hands clasping each other—she couldn't see them, because they'd sunk right into Leni's neck and disappeared from view.

Leni looked down at the ghostly arms emerging from her neck and began to shriek. "Get it off me! Get it off me! Shoo! Shoo!"

Cori ran over with his sword. "Unhand her, you foggy fiend!" he shrieked, "or I'll unhand you!" Then, with two swift cuts, he chopped off each of Lenora's hands at the wrist, leaving the hands buried in Leni's neck. Then he began dividing the rest of her into a larger number of separate parts, which floated in formation in the air in front of

Leni like a flock of birds for a moment before they rejoined.

Meanwhile, Coren rushed over and pulled on Cori, making odd noises like "ei ou ou aay on er." He too got chopped. For one brief moment, as Cori's sword cut wildly in all directions, pieces of Coren and pieces of Lenora collided wildly into each other, and Lenora suddenly found herself thinking, Let go of my fiancé, you stupid hunk of muscle! And get out of my room! I hate you, I hate you, I hate you! Finally, she managed to get hold of herself and began thinking her own thoughts—which nevertheless still seemed pretty scattered.

Sayley leaned against the door frame, watching, with an amused smile on her face. After a few moments, though, she seemed to decide she'd seen enough. She took a few steps into the room and pointed her finger toward Cori, who suddenly froze and stopped moving altogether, right in the middle of a leaping lunge. For a brief instant he stood there balanced on one foot, his entire body teetering back and forth even though no individual part of it moved at all. Finally, he fell to the floor with a resounding crash, his body still in the same position, his sword still in lunging position but now pointed straight upward. He looked very much like a statue of a duelist that someone had knocked over.

"So much for him," Sayley said, rubbing her hands together. "And If I were you, lady," she added, turning to Leni, "I'd sit down, stop screaming, and behave."

Leni merely stood and stared at her, a dazed expression on her face.

By now, all the parts of Lenora had coalesced back into a whole. She pulled her hands out from where they were buried in Leni's neck and found herself making a noise, which sounded like someone choking to death but was actually a laugh. Then she moved over to Sayley.

"Lenora," Sayley said, staring at, or more accurately, through her. "It is you, isn't it?"

Lenora nodded.

"What's happened?" Sayley asked. "What's wrong with you?"

"Oreh ah eye awin issoh!" Lenora said. Sayley just looked confused.

"Issoh?" she said. "What's an issoh?"

"Aw issoh! Issoh!" Impatiently, Lenora tried to think how she could communicate with Sayley. Then she remembered the poor Andillans in the village they'd gone through, the ones who'd had to communicate by gesture because they'd forgotten how to talk. Well, if they could do it, so could she.

She began to bounce up and down as if she were on a horse.

"Oh, dear," Sayley said. "Now you're starting to have convulsions or something! This is terrible!"

Lenora nodded her head impatiently. How could she get Sayley to understand. Maybe if both she and Coren were doing it?

Still pretending to be on a horse, she trotted over to Coren, who was looking down at the statue that had recently been Cori with a triumphant smile on his face. Still trotting, she motioned Coren to do the same. He just stood there and stared at her for a while, looking at her as if she was completely demented. Then he suddenly realized what she was doing and nodded, and he began trotting, too.

This is awful, Coren thought as he trotted. Here he was, completely transparent and pretending to be a horse, while that muscle-bound fool Cori took over *his* room! At least for now he was immobilized—it must have been that little girl Sayley who'd imagined Cori like that. He was beginning to like Sayley more and more.

But where was his body? Was it back there with no mind left in it? What if those people came to examine them and found them lying there, vacant eyed, empty? Maybe they'd think they were *dead*. Maybe they'd bury them in the ground, and then, when they found some way to pull themselves together again and their minds returned—

Coren tried not to panic and began to gallop even faster. They had to get Sayley to understand. "Ayyyyyy!" he shrieked. It was as close as he could get to a neigh.

"I get it!" Sayley finally said. "It's like charades. You're being horses, right?"

Coren and Lenora both nodded enthusiastically and galloped and neighed harder.

"A horse swallowed you up! No, a horse trampled on you and pushed your minds out of your bodies! No, a horse—"

It took them some time to get Sayley to understand about the trip on horseback, and the locked room took even longer. Coren found himself remembering an awful mime who'd entertained at a banquet in Gepeth once, and nearly put them all to sleep pretending to be inside an invisible box. He tried it.

Luckily, Sayley had a higher tolerance for mime than he did.

"You're prisoners somewhere," she said. "That's excellent, Coren. I can see it so clearly!" She thought for a minute. "And Lenora, I suppose you tried to imagine yourselves back here, but it didn't quite work. Because your powers aren't quite working. Right, Lenora? Aren't I right?"

Coren had to admit that Sayley was one smart little kid.

"Surely," Leni said, "that awful scary thing isn't Lenora?" Leni had been doing her best to get Cori up off the floor—a difficult task when he seemed to have turned to solid stone. She now stood with him in her arms as he teetered precariously on one foot, holding on to him for dear life so that he wouldn't crash down to the floor again.

"Oh, dear," Sayley said as she looked back over her shoulder toward Leni. "I'd forgotten all about him." She blinked her eyes, and Cori suddenly melted back into himself again. For a moment he looked disoriented, unsure of where he was. Then he realized that Leni was embracing him.

"Leni!" he cried. "Smooching! What a terrific idea!" And he reached over and gave her a big kiss.

"Gross," Sayley said. "And in public, too." She blinked again, and both Cori and Leni became statues. If somebody didn't do something, that kiss was going to go on forever.

"Uuuuughhh," Coren said.

"Yeeeeccch," Lenora added.

"Now that," Sayley said, "I can understand. And I totally agree." She blinked again, and Leni and Cori came to life—and kept right on kissing anyway—for an astonishingly long time.

"Ooh, Cori-worri," Leni finally said in a breathless voice. "That was scrumptious."

"Yes, indeed," he said. "I'm good at *that*, too. Knights always are."

"Look, you two," Sayley barked. "That's enough of that mushy stuff. Okay?"

They looked at her, fear in their eyes.

"Okay," they said, guiltily letting go of each other.

"Good. Because we have to help Lenora here." She gestured toward the ghostly presence.

"That really is Lenora?" Leni asked.

"Yes."

Leni approached more closely and stared into the cloud. "Yes," she said, "now that I look more closely, I can see the split ends. It *is* Lenora."

"I think so," said Sayley. "And that one with the sunset on

top and the blue guck in the middle, that's Coren. And we have to help them."

"I'll rescue them," said Cori, rushing over and waving his sword about. "So what if they're stuck up, stick-in-the-mud, no-fun people without a noble thought in their heads? So what if that cowardly no-muscled varlet Coren deserves to be drawn and quartered and have the remains of his pusillanimous carcass pecked by vultures and then made into soup for beggars! I'm a brave knight, I am! Sir Cori the Brave! And we brave knights will use *any* excuse to do something brave—even a poor excuse like those two cloudy things. So let's go! At it, at it, at it!"

"Oh, Cori," whimpered Leni, "you're so wonderful! I'll come, too, of course, because I'm a lady, and a lady must go everywhere her brave knight goes! Just give me a day or two to pack, and we'll be on our way!"

A day or two? Lenora, hovering vaguely in front of Sayley, could hardly believe what she was hearing. There was no way she could be separated from her body for a day or two. She needed her body. And anyway, why were they planning to travel at all, when Leni could or Sayley just imagine them back here in a blink of an eye?

Well, thank goodness for Sayley at least. The little girl had some brains—she could talk some sense into these two idiots and calm them down in no time. And then she herself would do the sensible thing and imagine them back here.

"That's just it," Sayley said, not getting worried. "We can't go there, because we don't know where to go! What will we do?"

"Oh, ayee," Lenora said. "Oh oo see? All oo ah ooo oo ih ih ah in ih!"

But Sayley wasn't paying any attention to her. The three of

them, Sayley and Leni and Cori, had only one thing on their minds. They seemed to be determined to go out and find the rest of her and Coren when they didn't even know where to look.

Well, Lenora sighed, if they had to go, they had to go. She floated herself over in front of Sayley and began to mimic being on a horse again.

Sayley smiled. "Of course," she said to Lenora, "I'll get a horse and you'll ride on it with me. What's left of you. You can show me which way to go!"

Lenora nodded enthusiastically.

"But," Sayley said hesitantly, "what about Coren? There really isn't room for three on a horse, no matter how little of you there is."

"Don't forget I'm coming," Cori said. "To protect you from harm and slay things. The cowardly varlet can ride with me."

"And I'm coming, too," Leni said. "To watch Cori triumph over the evil enemy. As soon as I pack. Just wait—I'll only be three or four hours, I promise. Not a minute over five!" And she rushed out of the room.

"Well," Sayley said, an ironic smile on her face, "that gets rid of her. Let's go."

CHAPTER 13

They managed to sneak out of the castle without anyone seeing them. The more Lenora thought about it the happier she was that Sayley had shown up like that. Her parents and Coren's parents could have taken days having meetings, consulting with advisors, figuring out the best thing to do and exactly what or who these apparitions really were. But Sayley was like Lenora herself—all action. That's why she liked the little girl so much.

It was hard to sit on the horse, though, because her hands couldn't hold on to Sayley and her feet and legs couldn't hold on to the horse. There just wasn't enough substantial to hang on to anything—she kept sliding off the back end and then had to part jump, part float back on again.

Coren, meanwhile, had given up on sitting on the horse altogether. For one thing, he didn't like being that close to Cori, and not just because he couldn't stand the numbskull. The odor that emanated from Cori made it clear that he had spent his day as usual, lifting weights and jogging and doing whatever other mindless activities he could dream up to fill the time that normal people would have spent thinking. He smelled worse than the refuse containers they were all heading toward. Besides which, his armor had points sticking out of it, and even though Coren couldn't really feel them in his current condition, the thought of actually leaning against them made him very uncomfortable. It was like hugging a set of carving knives.

All things considered, it was better to travel by himself. Luckily, he'd discovered he was so light that, every time he took a step, he bounded high into the air and came down some distance farther down the road. It was an easy matter to bound on ahead of the horses and show them the way—and not the least bit tiring.

Watching Coren from where she had fallen behind Sayley's horse yet once more, Lenora quickly realized the wisdom of his technique, and propelled herself in his direction with a mighty hop. Soon they were bounding along together, leading the others down the same route they'd taken that morning, through the now-sleeping dilapidated village and, finally, to the borders of the strange town.

Sayley and Cori left their horses at the edge of town and silently followed their ghostly guides down the now-deserted streets.

"This is really odd," said Cori as they walked. "How could this town be here? I have no memory at all of a town like this in Andilla."

"Shush," said Sayley. "Let's just get them back to their bodies."

Finally the spirits of Coren and Lenora stopped, just down the block from the large white building with the wide green door, and pointed across the street. The boy Mud was sitting there on the ground, leaning against the door, and he seemed to be asleep.

Lenora bounded over to where Sayley could see her clearly and pretended to be reaching into her pocket.

"I get it," Sayley said. "A key—he has a key."

Lenora nodded and put her finger over her mouth.

"Don't worry," Sayley whispered, "I'll be very quiet. I'll just creep over there and—"

"Rise and shine, young rascal!" It was Cori's voice, booming across the night. He had already strode across the road and was jabbing at the sleeping boy with the point of his sword. "Bestir yourself, sirrah, and show us where Coren and Lenora are or I'll be forced to do my knightly duty and run you through!"

Mud awoke with a start, then stiffened as he noticed the sword digging into him and began to pull away from it, plastering himself up against the wall. Then, before anyone could quite figure out what was happening, Mud had suddenly rolled sideways and was up on his feet, holding a broom straight out in front of him and shouting, "Watch it, mister! I have a weapon! And I charge by the minute!"

"Oh no, you don't" said Cori, thrusting forward with his sword. "Take that, my loudmouthed lad."

Mud now held only the little that was left of the handle— the rest of the broom lay on the ground at his feet. "Destruction of civic property!" he said, horrified. "Twenty-three points!"

"Thank you ever so much, Cori," said Sayley who had marched across the square, Coren and Lenora bounding along behind her. "So much for the element of surprise."

"Who are you?" Mud said, ineffectually waving his stump of broom handle at Sayley. Then he noticed Coren and Lenora, or rather, what was left of them, leaning over each of Sayley's shoulders. Then he fainted.

Cori shook his head. "Coward," he sneered.

"Well, at least he stood up to you, Mr. Big Noise," Sayley said. "And with nothing but a broom, too. If you ask me, *you're* the coward—attacking a poor little kid like that."

That's telling him, Coren thought.

"Just who are you calling a coward, young miss?" Cori said menacingly, waving his sword in front of Sayley's nose. "Lucky for you you're a lady, sort of, or else I'd—"

"Oh, for heaven's sake," said Sayley. She made a small gesture toward the sword, which grew brown bristles all along its sharp edges. "That's odd," she said. "I meant to turn it into a broom. My powers aren't working quite right all of a sudden."

"Well enough to ruin my best sword. Turn it back this instant!" Cori demanded. But Sayley was ignoring him. She walked over to the unconscious boy and looked at him.

"Well," she sighed, "at least it makes it easier for us to find the keys."

It took only a few seconds for her to take the keys off Mud's belt and open the door, and only a few more to find a light switch. The vast room full of containers sprang into view.

"Pee-you," Sayley said. "This stuff smells almost as bad as you do, Cori."

Cori gave her a nasty look but said nothing.

By now, Coren could hardly wait to get his body back. He bounded over to where their two bodies sat on the floor, flopped against each other and staring blankly ahead. They looked like two huge dolls.

Then, without even thinking about what he was doing, he ran forward, and, with one last large bound, jumped feet first, right into the middle of his body.

Coren blinked. He could feel his eyelids actually go down and then come back again. He could see Sayley and Cori standing in front of him. He could feel pain in his arms and legs, which had been in the same positions for hours. Things were back to normal!

He watched Lenora as she copied what he had done. And then she was back in her body, too.

"Sayley," Lenora said, getting to her feet with a few groans. "Thank you!"

Sayley grinned.

Coren, now on his feet also, hobbled over to Sayley and gave her a hug. "That was a truly unpleasant experience," he commented. "And every muscle I own is cramped up."

"Mine, too," Lenora said. "But there's no time to worry about that now. Let's get out of here before the boy wakes up and alerts his entire town and we're *all* stuck here."

"Help! Help!" It was Mud. "Everyone, help! Twelve points for nocturnal succor, and a bonus for any weapons you can bring!"

"Too late," said Sayley. "I should have turned *him* into a broom."

"Never mind," Cori said, "we'll fight our way out! I am Sir Cori the Brave! I live for moments like this! I'll show you who's a coward and who isn't, once and for all! At it, at it, at it!" He rushed toward the door, wildly waving his sword in front of him. In his excitement, he seemed to have forgotten all about the bristles.

CHAPTER 14

"That won't be necessary," Sud Girth said as he strolled into the building, accompanied by a frantic Mud. "Y12," he said to Mud, "go get these people's horses." Mud nodded, then scooted out the door as fast as he could go.

"You're letting us go?" Lenora said, incredulous.

"Yes. No matter how much you owe us, you are just too erratic to keep around. Yesterday's disruptions, uproars in the middle of the night—you're ruining our schedules. People are getting behind in their work. People are feeling emotions, for heaven's sake. Why, even I—" He paused, a look of anguish on his face, then sighed deeply. "I hate to admit it, but I actually had a dream tonight, before I was so rudely awakened by yet more of your outrageous shenanigans. Me, Sud Girth O60, a dream! Unreal things happened in it—sheer unadulterated fantasies. It's not natural, I tell you, not natural at all."

Not natural to have a dream? These people were even more deranged than Lenora had been thinking. Could they actually be the source of all the problems? Could their inability to imagine somehow be swallowing up everyone's powers?

"In any case," Sud continued, "it's really not cost-effective to keep you here. I've never met such spendthrifts—you're totally out of control. Why, even locked up here in Refuse Holding you've managed to add a few hundred more points to your total. And then there's the consumables we'd have to waste on you, and the cost of guards, and the wear and tear on the facilities—don't think I didn't notice the dents in that container you knocked over, because I did. Forty points, that is—schedule 6543. No, it simply isn't worth it to keep you here. So, you're welcome to leave. In fact, you're ordered to leave, immediately."

"You mean I can't fight?" Cori said, miserably disappointed.

"No," said Sud. "Definitely not. No fighting. Not in this sector."

"Poo," Cori said. Then his face brightened. "I wouldn't charge you," he said. "I'd be happy to hew and hack my way out of here for free!" He brandished his broom-sword. "It'd be a truly magnificent spectacle—and I wouldn't charge you a single point!"

Sud ignored him. "You may leave immediately," he said. "But the terms of release are quite specific. I must know exactly what you are doing here. Why did you come in the first place, and why is it that you can actually see us Skwoes?"

"Skwoes?" Coren said. "Is that what you call yourselves?"
Sud nodded.

"Well," said Coren, "you see, our people have certain powers, which I don't think you have."

"Oh yes," said Sud, "we know all about you Swellheads. Live in your imaginations, never do an honest day's work, don't care what kind of squalor surrounds you."

"Hmph," Cori said menacingly. "Squalor indeed. Swellheads indeed. Impertinent varlet, I ought to—"

Coren quickly interrupted him. "Why is it," he asked, "that you know about us but we don't know about you?"

"Because we make it our business," said Sud, "to know about everything. Whereas you make it your business to have no business and to care about nothing. You just put everyone and everything but yourselves completely out of your minds."

Coren was insulted. "We care about each other!" he exclaimed.

Sud sniffed. "That's all as it may be," he said. "But you don't *do* anything, you don't produce anything, you have no idea about the real world."

"Our world is just as real as yours," Coren shot back, totally forgetting that Sud's words sounded exactly like the kinds of things he used to tell his parents and the Thoughtwatcher. "In its own way of course."

"Is it?" sneered Sud. "And do you know who makes the mush you live on?"

"No," said Coren, reluctant to admit it.

"We do."

"*You* do?"

"That's correct, young *prince*. We Skwoes grow the crop out in the fields—our fields. And then we process it here in Town Number One and deliver it to all you silly Swellheads in your Swellhead towns and castles. And take our fair and rightful payment for it, of course."

If what Sud was saying was true, Coren was even more bewildered than before. It meant these Skwoes had always been here, out in the Andillan countryside growing their crops and feeding his own people. Why had he never heard of them, never known they even existed? And what did Sud mean by a payment? Coren had never heard of Andillans ever paying for anything—they didn't even have money anymore.

"How can we pay you," he asked, "if we don't even know you exist?"

"With gold," Sud explained, "gold kept in storage receptacles just outside your towns and castles. The arrangement has been the same for hundreds of years. You've just forgotten. We pay ourselves out of it—and we're always absolutely fair about how much we take, so don't start thinking we'd cheat or anything—and it's the basis of our economy."

"Economy?" Coren asked. "What's that?"

"Sounds dangerous," Cori added. "I could kill it for you if you wanted."

Sud stared at them, then rolled his eyes. "Never mind. You'd never understand. Killing the economy, indeed—subversive thinking of the worst sort. But you still haven't answered my question. What are you doing here? And why can you see us? Usually when Swellheads wander into town they're so busy making things up in their useless heads that they don't even know we're there, and we can steer them right on out of town again without them even knowing we're doing it. How come *you* know?"

"Well," Coren said unhappily, "it seems we've lost our powers. We can't imagine anymore—hardly at all."

"I see. Without your powers, of course, you'd have to notice us. It's only logical, albeit exceedingly unusual behavior for a Swellhead."

Coren nodded. "Exceedingly. Princess Lenora and I, we were looking for the reason, when you grabbed us and stuck us in there. And then these others came along to rescue us."

"At it, at it, at it!" Cori shrieked. "Prince Cori the Brave to the rescue!"

"Rescue, indeed," said Sud. "You were just trying to get away without paying what you owe. Typical Swellhead self-indulgence. I might have known. Let's get moving."

As they made their way outside, Coren glared suspiciously at the Skwoe. He seem to hate people like Coren himself so much, to hate anyone who ever used their imagination. "Our losing our powers," he said, "you wouldn't happen to know anything about it, would you?"

"Of course not," Sud said, glaring right back at him. "Why would we? You Swellheads and your silly so-called powers mean less than nothing to us. Now just go back to your palace and don't come here again."

"But," said Lenora, "how do we *know* you have nothing to do with this? We only have *your* word for it, after all. And who are *you*, anyway?"

"I've told you, my name is Sud Girth, O60. Twenty points, not that I'll ever actually collect it. As for my title, I am head of this town. No offense to you, Mr. Prince, or whoever you think you are, but we have our own officials here. I bid for the job and won and I've been doing it for five years now."

"You bid for it?" Coren asked. "What does that mean?"

Sud shook his head impatiently. "Don't you know anything at all? I said I'd do it for twenty-five thousand points a year. Crud Blirth was my closest competition, but he bid twenty-six thousand—far too much, if you ask me. Crud has no sense of value. So naturally, I got it."

"So the person who offers to do the job for the least number of points runs the town?" Lenora asked.

"Correct."

"No matter how dumb he is? Even if he's terrible at running things?"

Sud glared at her angrily. At this point, fortunately, Mud returned, leading a procession of other boys all dressed in the same blue uniform who held the reins of both sets of their horses. Lenora, Coren, Cori, and Sayley each claimed a horse and jumped on.

Sud looked up at them for a moment with deep suspicion. Then he turned to Mud.

"Y12," he said, "I think you'd better go along with these people and make sure they do as they're told and return directly home. Climb up there on that horse with the little one." He pointed toward Sayley.

"Just try it," Sayley said, glaring at Mud menacingly. "Just go ahead and try."

Mud wasn't even listening to her. "Me?" he said to Sud. "Go *there*? I'm too young! It's too dirty! I'll lose all my shifts and be poor! No one will like me anymore! I *hate* horses! She's a girl! I don't want to!"

"Tsk, tsk," said Sud. "That'll be seven points for disrespect to an elder, with a bonus of two for a public official, for a total of nine. And twelve more for whining, which makes twenty-one. No, boy, you'll do as you're told, and that's that. Someone has to go, and I'm far too busy. Far too many strange things have been happening lately—why, even before these silly Swellheads showed up in A1 and disrupted everything, a group of M30s in Sector H4 were two minutes late for their exercise class yesterday. And five citizens on consumable duty in time Sector 5 actually stopped working and took a rest—said they were bored, of all things! And Glud Clirth of Sector J2 has decided to grow a mustache—a man who never had a counter-productive thought in his whole life before last Tuesday! Mustaches are not standard, not standard at all. And then there's my dream. Me, going fishing! Fishing is counter-societal! No, I can't leave, not in these circumstances. It'll have to be you, boy. Up you go."

Mud nodded unhappily and moved toward Sayley's horse.

"Just go ahead and try it," Sayley reiterated. "These boots have very sharp points." Mud gave her an alarmed look.

"In fact," Sud continued, "now that I think about it, you'd better stay with them for a few days and see what they're up to in that ridiculous filthy castle of theirs. Too many things are happening—and they've lost their powers, they say. It might be their fault, somehow, the mustache and the dream and all. It just might be. I want you there to keep an eye on them. Up you go."

By now Mud was standing beside Sayley's horse, looking straight into the sharp boot she was pointing toward his face.

"Are you their assistant?" he asked her defiantly. "I'll bet you don't earn half as much as me! I earn five thousand points a year! And I'm only twelve."

"Big deal," Sayley said, totally unimpressed. "I don't even know what a point is—although of course I could imagine what it is if I wanted to. I can imagine anything I want to. Can you?"

"Imagine? We don't imagine in Skwoeland. We don't *need* to imagine. And, anyway, it's very expensive."

"Not imagine?" Sayley scoffed. "Then you may as well be a rock or a tree."

"Sayley," Lenora interrupted. "Don't even try it. Just let him up on the horse." It might have been interesting to see Sud Girth's response if Sayley did indeed turn the boy into a tree, right before his boring, unimaginative eyes. But Lenora suspected it probably wouldn't have worked anyway, here in the Skwoe town—and there was no point in making the Skwoes even angrier than they were already. And, anyway, it was obvious that Sud wasn't going to let them go unless the boy came with them. They might as well get it over with.

"But, Lenora," Sayley whined. "It's just a small horse. There's no room! He's a boy! He has no imagination! Do I *have* to?"

"Yes, Sayley. You have to."

With a huge sigh, Sayley moved her foot. "Well, all right," she said. "But I still don't want to. Just don't you dare touch me," she added, "or you may find yourself feeling even more woodenheaded than you already are. If you get my meaning, which you probably don't."

Mud climbed into the saddle, reaching behind him to grab on to the edge, doing his best to keep some distance between himself and the girl in front of him.

"Don't worry," he said, "I don't *want* to touch you!" He could be heard mumbling something about a filthy Swellhead as the horses headed off down the street and he teetered precariously and held on for dear life.

CHAPTER 15

By the time they arrived back at the castle, dawn was breaking. Cori rushed off to find his beloved Leni and tell her of his heroic exploits (by now, in his mind, the Skwoes had turned into vengeful monsters with many-pointed claws, and Cori himself had single-handedly conquered them all by sweeping them off their feet with his mighty giant broom-sword and then punching them into submission). The rest of the group headed off to the main dining hall. Lenora wanted to see if her powers had returned now that they were away from the unimaginative Skwoes, so she imagined up a huge breakfast.

It worked. They had just started to dig into the hotcakes and hot buns and fresh butter and fresh fruit and steaming hot coffee when King Arno and Queen Milda rushed into the room.

"What?" said Arno "More buns, Lenora? I'm starting to be very insulted. Have some of mine." He thrust a basket of fresh baked buns toward her. She took a bite of one of his and decided that her own were better.

"Coren!" Queen Milda squeaked. She ran over and enveloped him in a huge embrace—a surprise for Coren, because his mother wasn't usually so demonstrative. He rather liked it. He hugged her back.

"Where have you been, lad?" King Arno asked, coming over and patting him on the back so enthusiastically that he nearly choked the breath out of him. "We couldn't find you anywhere. Have a bun."

"We've been worried, Coren darling," Queen Milda added. "Terribly worried."

Quickly Coren swallowed his bun and reassured his parents, and then told them about the expedition out into the country-side and all that he and Lenora had discovered. They both seemed quite shaken.

"You say they live right here, in our land?" King Arno asked.

"And they speak aloud," asked Milda. "In *voices*?"

"See for yourself," said Coren, and he led them over to where Mud stood silently in a corner, looking suspiciously at the plate of hotcakes and syrup he held in one hand and the fork he held in the other.

"This tastes very good," he was saying angrily to Sayley. "I'm enjoying it."

"If you're enjoying it," she said, "why do you sound so angry?"

"Because I can't afford to enjoy anything, of course. Do you know how many hundreds of points that is? Self-indulgence is almost as bad as amusement. I'll be broke for months. No one will like me." Miserably, he took another bite of a hotcake.

Sayley looked at him in disbelief and shook her head back and forth. "There's not even any point in turning you into a rock," she said. "Rocks aren't half as thick."

When Coren introduced Mud to the king and queen, he didn't bow or seem impressed in any way. He just stared at them and their tattered clothes and looked like he would rather be anywhere else, then took another bite of the hotcakes.

"What do you call yourself, lad?" King Arno asked nicely. "Have a bun."

"Mud Sirth Y12. Twenty points, that is. And I can't afford a bun."

"No, your other name. A Schmo, was it?"

"A Skwoe, you mean?"

"A Skwoe!" King Arno marveled.

"A Skwoe?" echoed another voice, greatly alarmed. It was the Thoughtwatcher, who had just come into the room.

"Oh, hello, Kaylor," said Arno. "Have a bun. You know about these Skwoes?"

"Yes," she said grimly. "I do. What is he doing here in the castle?"

After Coren filled her in on their trip out to the countryside and explained Mud's presence, she shook her head sadly. "It's worse than I thought," she said.

"What do you mean?" Coren asked.

"What do you mean?" echoed Milda. "And why have you never told us about these Skwoe things?" She gestured distastefully at Mud, who continued to glower at her as he sucked his syrup-covered fingers.

"Well," Kaylor said, "I probably shouldn't be telling you this. But things have gone haywire already as it is, and I suppose you need to know. I've read about them, you see. In the Precious Recordings of the Great Histories. Praise the Recordings."

"Praise them," said Coren automatically, and everyone else but Mud echoed his words. "What did you read?"

"About the Skwoes. According to the Precious Recordings, the people of this land were greatly divided about how they wanted to live, back in the Days of Agreement when the divine Letishia appeared."

"Letishia?" Sayley said excitedly. "I know all about her! It's really Le—!"

"Never mind, Sayley," said Lenora. She really didn't like to think about her own involvement with the famous ancestress Letishia. "Now is not the time. Go on, Thoughtwatcher."

"Some of us Andillans wanted to have the power of thought. Others distrusted anything imaginative. So an agreement was made. Half of the Andillans would live one way, half the other—and in that way, there would be balance. The Equilibrium would be maintained."

To Lenora, it seemed very strange indeed. Back home in Gepeth, each and every individual person had to maintain the Balance in themselves. But here, it seemed, every individual had to go to an extreme, be either totally imaginative or totally unimaginative, in order to keep the whole country in balance. You had to be unbalanced for the sake of the Balance.

"Hmmm," said Coren thoughtfully. "It does make sense."

"Of course it does," said Kaylor. "It's in the Recordings. It's the way thing are and have to be. Which, young man, is why *your* strange behavior was always so dangerous. For every court Andillan who imagines, there is a Skwoe who doesn't—so when you refused to use your powers, it upset the Balance. And who knows?" She gave Coren an angry look. "Maybe that was when all this chaos began, with your silly little childish games. When it comes to Equilibrium, small things lead to big things, and big things to even bigger ones."

Coren felt himself turn red. Could it really be possible? Could he have been the one who started all these horrible problems, just by refusing to live the life of the mind?

So, Lenora thought, another suspect to add to my list—which now, with the addition of Coren, included just about everybody she knew and a few more besides. And the more people there were on the list, the less likely it was that she herself had been responsible. As much as she cared for Coren, she'd even be grateful if it turned out to be him—as long as it wasn't Lenora herself for a change. She was tired of being the problem all the time. Let Coren suffer a little.

"In any case," Kaylor continued, "the Recordings are perfectly clear. For the Equilibrium to be maintained, there must be a complete and absolute separation between the two different peoples of Andilla. We who have powers have put the Skwoes completely out of our minds—and except for the mush exchange, the Skwoes steer clear of our places and keep us out of theirs. That boy should not be here—no more than you people should have knowingly gone to the Skwoe town. That's what the Precious Recordings say. Praise them."

"The Precious Recordings?" It was the Keeper Agneth, who had just come into the room. "Praise the Precious Recordings! Praise the Balance!"

"Praise the Balance! Praise the Equilibrium!" everyone murmured.

"Have a bun, Keeper," Arno added.

The Keeper eyed the plate suspiciously, then turned to Kaylor.

"But I trust, Thoughtwatcher," he said, "that you have undergone the Baths of Purification? And said the Rituals of the Opening before you spoke of the Recordings? Remember the Balance!"

"That's about all I *can* do, these days," Kaylor said bitterly. "Remember it—because it certainly isn't much in evidence around here. Powers gone, Skwoes at court, buns being made by everybody in sight—I can't see how a little water in a tub is going to make all that much difference."

"You didn't!" Agneth said in horror. "You didn't actually speak of divine matters in an unpurified state?"

Kaylor nodded.

For a moment the speaker just stared at her in disbelief. "Has everyone," he said, "gone completely and totally crazy? Everyone in the entire known universe? I can't—I won't—"

Then his face changed. His eyes glazed over, and his mouth curled into a strange, unsettling smile as he reached down and grabbed his left foot with his left hand and then began to hop on the other leg. As Lenora watched in horror, Agneth hopped himself right out of the room, still smiling that peculiar smile.

Oh, dear, Lenora thought. Watching the Keeper hop on one leg was like watching her mother throw mud on a carpet. After all, Agneth was the Keeper, the Keeper of the Balance. The fact that he was so out of balance suggested just how serious the situation was, even more serious than she'd imagined. Something had to be done, and soon.

What I need, she told herself, is a pencil and some paper. Then I could actually write my list down, and do some careful thinking about it. Slowly, so that no one else would notice her doing it, she moved her arm to behind her back where no one could see, and made a pad of paper and a pencil appear in it.

The paper and pad that appeared were almost as upsetting as Agneth's hopping. The paper was a hideous mauve color, the pencil about a foot long and rather rubbery. No doubt about it, the lack of balance was getting worse, her powers becoming more and more erratic.

Well, at least the bendy pencil was still usable. She crept over to the other side of the room where no one would see her and began to write down names.

"Lenora," she put at the top of the list. Then she frowned, quickly crossed it out, and wrote, in capital letters, "COREN." She could feel the smile appear on her face.

Meanwhile, everyone else had surrounded Mud and was throwing questions at him. They were learning far more than they could possibly need to know about how many points it cost to appear in public in Sectors 1 through 8 without your hat, and how many consumables subsector Y45 was responsible for in each time sequence before attracting the lateness penalty.

It all seemed very boring to Lenora, whose head was filled with mysterious possibilities. "Leni," she wrote. And then, "Skwoes." And hey, how about Agneth? Maybe his breakdown was the cause of all this, and not just the result of it—maybe it had been happening for some time without them even noticing it. He had always seemed pretty deranged to Lenora. "Agneth," she wrote, with a star beside it.

And the Thoughtwatcher—she'd told them things they weren't supposed to know and consulted the Precious Recordings without purifying herself. And then, of course, there was Sayley. She had such a strong will. Of course, Sayley wouldn't cause all this damage on purpose, but—

But if Sayley could do it unconsciously, so could Lenora herself. Sighing, she wrote her own name back down again, in very small letters. Then, after staring at it for a while, she put a very large question mark after it.

By this point, the names were all buzzing around each other in her head. SayleyCorenLeniLenora. She'd had a hectic day, and she hadn't slept all night, so it wasn't surprising that she was so tired. CorenArnoAngnethSayleyLenoraLenoraLenora. Lenora so very tired, LenoraLenora so completely and—

"Lenora Lenora Lenora!"

It is gray. A mist rises from the ground. She wades through it, as if it is a field of grain she is pushing through. She is trying to get somewhere. But where?

"Lenora. Here. I'm here. Come to me."

It's Hevak. He's evil, of course. But his voice sounds so sweet. So compelling. She has to go. She moves farther forward. And then, the mists part and she sees him. Tall, broad shouldered, black wavy hair, chiseled features, gleaming white teeth, full smile.

"Ah! Lenora! There you are! I've been calling you. Calling you."

He is surrounded by a soft golden glow. "Come to me. I'm different now. I've changed. Come to me."

She moves closer and closer. There is a sweet scent like lemon blossoms all around him, so clean, so clean and good.

Goodness. That's what she wants. Goodness everywhere. A perfect world.

Isn't Hevak evil, though? Yes, she must pull back, she must—

But he doesn't look evil or smell evil or seem evil. Of course, he never did. For a moment Lenora struggles with that thought. But she is drawn, drawn . . .

"Oh! Lenora, wake up! Wake up right now!"

It is Sayley, pulling on her hands so forcefully that she is actually drawing her up off the chair and onto her feet. She shakes her head to clear it.

"That Mud boy is really too much! He got your mother so upset she imagined he was a towel. Now she can't get him back properly. You'd better come."

CHAPTER 16

"Oh, Lenora," Queen Savet said as Sayley, holding tightly on to Lenora's hand, pulled her over to the group on the other side of the room. "I really didn't mean to do it! Only he was upsetting Milda here when your father and I came in, and I was just sort of thinking how much better I'd like him if he were a nice clean, quiet towel you could fold and put away in a closet instead of an annoying boy who had no imagination whatsoever who refused to answer questions, and suddenly he was gone and there's the towel." She pointed toward a plain brown towel, which sat folded on the table. "A very plain sort of towel, too," she added. "I've already folded it."

"But why can't you and father bring him back?" Lenora asked, concerned. Then she noticed Sayley. "Or you?" she added.

The king, the queen, and the little girl all just stared down at their feet.

"Do you mean that you, Father, *and* Sayley don't have enough power between you to return him to himself?"

King Rayden shrugged. "We tried."

"All that happened was that the towel got bigger," said Sayley. "And browner."

"And I had to fold it all over again," Savet added.

Lenora knew that her powers were greater than each one of them individually—even Sayley. But all together? This was getting even more serious. Were their powers about to disappear altogether, just like the Andillans?

"I think we'd better try together," she said.

And they did. Boy, they thought. Not towel, boy. Mud. They all thought very hard. The towel began to wriggle a little, but then it slumped back down on the table. Then it wiggled again, and turned into a sloppy pile of mud—and then, once more, back into a towel again.

In a panic, Lenora concentrated on it with all her might. Boy, boy, boy, boy. Suddenly the towel disappeared and Mud appeared in its place, lying in a contorted heap on the table, folded up just as the towel had been. And despite all of Lenora's concentration, he was still covered in brown towel material where his blue suit used to be.

"Oof," he said, his hands trying to unwind themselves from his legs. "This hurts."

After Coren and Sayley helped him to unfold himself, Mud looked around, bewildered. "What happened?"

"Well, dear," said Queen Savet, "it was my fault really, but you weren't being very nice to my friend and your queen—"

"She's *not* my queen," Mud interrupted. "I'm a Skwoe."

"Oh!" said Queen Milda, almost breathless, staring at Mud in disbelief. "Not your queen? My heart is palpitating! Oh."

"There, you see," Queen Savet said to Mud. "It's that sort of remark that tends to upset a sovereign."

Mud tried to climb down from the table with as much dignity as possible. "I don't know what just happened," he said, "but I was actually thinking I might be a towel or something. And I'm not a towel, am I? Of course not. I'm thinking things that aren't true. That's imagination, that's what that is! It's expensive, and I don't like it. I feel ill. I think it's time for me to go back home."

Sayley snorted. "Good riddance to bad rubbish, if you ask me!"

"Nobody did ask you," Mud said. "Did they?"

"It's just an expression," Sayley said. "Honestly!"

"People should say what they mean," Mud said. "Even silly little girls with no sense."

"No sense? No sense? Why, I have more sense in my little finger than you have in your whole huge ugly head."

"That's impossible," Mud said. "Fingers don't have sense. They're just fingers is all. Don't you know anything?"

For a moment, Sayley just stared at him, her eyes icy. Then she held up her middle finger in front of him.

"Oh yeah?" The finger said through the little mouth that appeared on it. "So explain why I'm talking to you, Mr. Know-it-all rock-head Skwoe?" Then the finger made a vulgar gesture.

Sayley turned to Lenora, grinning. "I got *that* to work!"

"I can't take anymore," Mud declared. "Fingers can't talk. I am not a towel. I'm going home." He began to head for the door.

While Sayley and Mud had been having this discussion, the four monarchs and the Thoughtwatcher had been conferring together. Now they nodded and turned to Mud.

"Just a minute, young-ingrate-who-doesn't-have-a-queen," Queen Milda said.

"We want a word with you, sonny," King Rayden added.

"Come over here and have a bun," King Arno said.

"Now," Queen Savet chimed in imperiously.

Mud turned and looked at them.

"I'm going home, and that's that."

"Yes, of course," said Rayden. "We *want* you to go home."

"In fact," said Milda, "We *order* you to."

"And take a message from us," said Savet.

"Yes," said Kaylor. "Tell your people that we here at the castle don't want mush anymore."

"Mush is so boring when you can't think it into something else," Milda said. "We want real food, like you eat yourselves. You wouldn't happen to have any dragon flambé lying around, would you?"

"And also," Savet said, "we'll need some of your people to come to the castle. It really has to be fixed and cleaned up. The rest of the wedding guests will begin to arrive any minute now."

"And from what it says in the Recordings," Kaylor added, "when it comes to getting things in order, you Skwoes are the ones to do it. Dreadfully and completely practical, you are."

"It'll have to be done quickly, too," Arno said. Tell your people just to drop everything and come here at once, on order of the king. Me, that is—*King* Arno."

Coren looked at his father in astonishment. He had never heard him pull rank like that before on an Andillan. True, he *was* the King, but that only meant that he had the responsibility to make sure everything was running smoothly and the Balance was in order. Coren had never heard him order anyone about before.

Lenora too seemed slightly taken aback. Her parents were just guests here in Andilla. They were behaving very badly. She opened her mouth to object when her father spoke. "And Lenora, you will kindly keep your opinions to yourself. This is Andillan business, best left to the king and queen."

Lenora stuck her elbow in Coren's ribs. "*You* say something, then," she demanded.

"Uh," Coren said, "Mother, Father, may I speak to you *privately*."

"Later, dear," Queen Milda said. "You, unmannerly Skwoe lad—you run along now."

"I'm going," Mud said. "Right now. I'm already gone. You

can expect my bill." He turned on his heel and stalked out of the room.

"Good," said Rayden. "We'll soon have some order back! After all, if we can't imagine food or nice quarters we'll have to do it another way. It's lucky you discovered the Skwoes," he said to Coren.

Lenora could contain herself no longer. Never mind the glare from both her father and her mother.

"You shouldn't be ordering the Skwoes about!" she exclaimed. "We should be trying to figure out what's causing all of this. I mean, it's obvious that whatever it is, is also starting to affect us Gepethians or you wouldn't have needed my help to change Mud back from being a towel."

Queen Savet scolded her. "Lenora, you apologize immediately!"

"No," Lenora said. "I *can't* apologize. After all, what I said is true. Right, Coren?"

Coren took a deep breath. He hated arguments and confrontations as much as Lenora loved them. But he knew she was right.

"She's right," Coren said glumly, knowing how angry his parents would be. "We can't just order people about—the Skwoes don't even recognize you as king and queen."

"What we have to do," Lenora said, "is find out *why* this is happening." She took Coren by the arm. "And that's just what we're going to do. Figure it out."

She stalked out of the room, pulling Coren along with her.

"They've all gone completely out of their minds," she muttered. "And we'd better find out the cause or we'll be next!"

CHAPTER 17

When they reached Coren's room, Lenora remembered she had a confession to make.

"Uh, Coren, that's not exactly your room," she said.

Quickly, and greatly embarrassed, she told him how she had duplicated the room for Leni and Cori, and hidden his real room behind a secret panel. "It's just down there," she added, pointing a little down the hallway.

For a moment, Coren merely stared at her. Then he shook his head and walked over to the panel.

"Just press that flower," Lenora said.

The moment Coren touched the flower, an entire section of the wall just the size of a door swung open—and as it did, it was replaced by a wall of water that completely filled the opening. The water wall held for only the briefest of instants, a mere flick of the eye, then began to pour out of the door all at once in a huge, powerful wave. The wave caught up Coren, his finger still on the flower, and before Lenora could reach out for him, he had been swept off his feet and dragged down the corridor and almost out of her view.

By that point, though, the force of the water had diminished, and Coren came to a quick and painful halt, his movement stopped by a particularly large tuck in the carpet. He lay there like a beached whale, sopping wet and gasping and coughing up water.

Lenora herself had been standing just on the edge of the

wave. The water had sloshed up over her feet and up to her ankles, but the rest of her was completely dry.

Oops, thought Lenora. She'd gotten so tired waiting for the water yesterday morning, so that she could brush her teeth—Coren had told her it took a long time to come, but not *that* long. Finally, she'd simply imagined her own water. I suppose, she thought, I must have forgotten to turn off the real tap. And eventually, obviously, the water did start to run—and had been running ever since.

Coren did not look happy.

"All right, Lenora," he said angrily, running his hand through his hair in order to get rid of some of the water, "what have you done now? Because I know you've done something. This"—he made a sweeping gestured down the corridor, causing a heavy rainfall of droplets all over Lenora—"this has all your earmarks."

Sheepishly, Lenora told him.

He climbed to his feet and shook himself like a dog. "Let's go look at the damage," he said, his voice resigned.

The room was a soggy mess. Everything was soaking wet and dripping. The furniture had floated out of position and landed helter-skelter. The table was on the bed frame, the mattress on the other side of the room. The color of the drapes had run, and there were maroon puddles on everything—including what was left of the books and papers. The room Coren had worked so hard on now looked exactly like the rest of the castle.

"Ruined," Coren said, giving her an accusing look. "Totally ruined."

"I could fix it for you, I know I could, Coren. Just let me—"

He turned to her, fire in his eyes. "Oh no! No, you don't! I won't have you change a single thing. I built this room without once using my powers, and I'm going to build it again, in exactly the same way. You just keep your awful imagination out of here!"

Lenora really did feel dreadful. It was pathetic to watch Coren slogging sadly around the room, uncovering more evidence of serious damage every minute. When she went into the bathroom to turn off the still-running tap, Coren's voice dripped with irony. "Oh, thank you ever so much, Lenora," he said. "Actually turning off the tap you turned on! How ever so kind of you. You *are* such a helpful person."

"I really am sorry, Coren," she said. "It *was* thoughtless. I know how hard you worked on this room."

Coren was staring at a book, all blotted now and unreadable. "What's that?" she asked.

"Just my journal," Coren replied, a tear appearing in the corner of his eye.

"Oh no," she exclaimed. He had told her all about that journal, on more than one occasion. She knew how very much it mattered to him.

But then she had an idea. "Coren," she said, "I promise I won't imagine anything for you here, nothing at all, I swear it. It's your room, and I'll let you handle it if that's what you want. But you're never going to be able to rewrite that journal all over again."

"I know," he said mournfully. "It's lost. All my memories, all my ideas, all my fantasies, lost forever."

"But that's the thing. The journal isn't lost."

"Huh?"

"Remember the other room? The one I made for Cori? It's the exact duplicate of this one—including your journal. We could go there and get it. Or," she added as a thought struck her, "if you'd rather not go there and be reminded of, well, everything, I could go myself."

"Oh no," he said, leaping to his feet, "I'm not taking any more chances. It's my journal! You just keep your hands off it! I'll go get it myself."

Well, she thought, as she raced down the hall after him, hopping over puddles and hills in the carpet, at least he didn't seem to be worried about that journal in the other room being a product of her imagining. Strange how inconsistent people are when it comes to things that really matter to them.

By the time Lenora made it through the door, Coren was already over by the nightstand, down on his knees, opening drawers and flipping through papers.

"Hey!" Cori was saying. "What do you think you're doing? I just swept this floor in my magnificently excellent knightly fashion, and you're tracking muddy water all over it. And let me tell you it isn't easy to sweep with this thing." He held aloft his sword with bristles emerging from each side of the blade. "What are you doing in *my* drawers anyway?"

"Honestly, Coren," said Leni, who was sitting primly on the bed applying polish to her fingernails. "You're spattering my Dawn Blush. It'll dry unevenly."

Coren paid no attention to them at all. "Here it is," he shouted. "My journal!"

"That's *my* journal," said Cori. "And watch out, you're getting it wet. The ink will run and then I won't be able to read it anymore."

He rushed over and tried to grab the journal out of Coren's hands. Coren pulled back.

"Now look, you two," said Lenora. "If you don't stop, you're going to rip it in half."

Coren immediately realized she was right and stopped pulling, so the journal stayed in Cori's hands. He held it aloft triumphantly. "Victory is mine!" he said. "To the victor go the spoils! Huzzah for Prince Cori the Brave!" Coren looked up at it longingly.

"Tell me, Cori," asked Lenora. "Are you actually planning ever to read that journal?"

"Of course not. Don't be silly. Knights don't read. It's not manly, reading."

Nor, apparently was thinking. "Well, then," she said, "why not let Coren have it?"

"Because it's mine!" he said. "I won!"

"But wouldn't you rather have—oh, let's say, a new sword to replace that one with the bristles?"

Cori immediately got a crafty gleam in his eye. "Would it have a serrated titanium edge and a Snetzerland flesh-entering finish?"

"It could be arranged. Just give Coren the journal."

"A Snetzerland flesh-entering finish! Okay!" He tossed the journal to Coren, who caught it and cradled it as close to his chest as he could get it without actually soaking it. Coren didn't seem the least bit worried that it was, yet once more, Lenora's imagining that had got it for him.

"But," Cori added, "I'll want a handle of Kitznoldian oak, Lenora—handcarved."

"Yes, yes," said Lenora, "anything you want. But I'm not making it until the wedding is over—we've had quite enough swordplay around here lately, thank you."

"Yes, indeed," said Leni. "And enough water, too. How did you two get so wet? Your hair looks even worse than usual, Lenora."

"Never mind," said Lenora quickly. "What's been going on here?"

"Oh, Lenora, it's just ever so awful!" Leni said. "Just look! My brave Cori, a noble, manly hero, doing menial work. Sweeping, of all things!"

"But," Cori said with a self-satisfied smile, "I sweep very well. Don't I, milady?"

"Of course you do," said Leni. "I wouldn't expect any less, my knight. By the way, though, Cori, you've missed an entire spider's web—in that corner over there."

"A spider's web?" he said anxiously. "Where? Ah, I see it!" He jabbed the broom-sword at it. "Take that, you leggy varlet," he said. "Make way for Sir Cori the Brave!"

"That's much better, Cori darling. But oh, dear, oh, dear. After this"—Leni gestured at the puddles Coren and Lenora had made—"you'll be forced to *wash* the floor. Probably on your manly hands and knees. Tsk, tsk, tsk."

"Tsk, tsk," agreed Lenora.

"But," Leni told Lenora, "there you go. There's no choice, really, because I simply can't live in this squalor. And naturally"—she giggled—"my Cori won't allow *me* to ruin my nails or mess up my lovely gown, so he has to do it all himself, poor fellow. Why, it's practically torture to watch him." She nodded her head back and forth, a tragic expression on her face.

"It must have driven you crazy, Leni dear, living in all this filth." Lenora pretended sympathy in the hope that Leni might give away something.

It worked.

"You're right," Leni said confidentially, "it did! Don't forget that puddle over there by the dresser, Cori dear. In fact, Lenora—*please* don't tell Agneth, but, well, there have been times lately when I've been *forced* to use my powers, absolutely forced, just to eat something other than that awful mush, or so I could have a hot bubble bath! I simply couldn't survive without a hot bubble bath!"

"No," agreed Lenora, "I suppose you couldn't. Which means"—her voice changed in tone—"that it might have been you. You *were* willing to use your powers. And you might have got rid of the Andillan's powers just to force them to see what a mess this place is and get them to clean it up. What do you think, Coren? Isn't that logical?"

"Huh?" By this time, Coren had wiped his hands dry on the bedspread and was sitting on the floor and leafing through his journal, totally engrossed in his memories. "A dream about little colored dogs and white bears—I'd forgotten all about that! Whatever you say, Lenora."

"I'm hurt," said Leni, sniffling and on the verge of tears. "How could you think such an awful thing, just because I've been weak a couple of times. I wouldn't do it, I couldn't. What would Agneth say?"

Agneth, thought Lenora, is too busy hopping around on one foot to be thinking much of anything. And everyone else is equally useless, too involved in their own problems to see how serious things were. Even Coren had other things on his mind.

Not that it was his fault, of course—she did feel really dreadful about his room. So typical of her to be thoughtless like that. Why, now she had Leni upset, too. She should be so much better.

She *could* be so much better. A voice inside her said she could. A sharp, strong, clear voice.

Suddenly, she felt exhausted. She had to lie down.

She eyed Cori's bed. "I think I'll just . . . ," she murmured as she plopped down on the bed, her head swimming.

And then she was out.

CHAPTER 18

"Lenora?" Coren bent over her, worried. It was odd that she would just drop off like that, very odd. "Lenora?"

She didn't respond. He took her in his arms and raised her a little and gave her a gentle shake. Nothing. He shook harder. Still nothing. She was *fast* asleep. Something was very wrong.

"Hmh," she suddenly mumbled. She was talking—talking in her sleep. But what was she saying? It was so hard to make out.

Once more, Coren bent his ear to her face.

"I AM YOU!" she suddenly shouted, right into Coren's ear. He pulled back in pain, then stared down at her still sleeping form in bewilderment.

It had not been Lenora's voice, shouting like that and nearly breaking his eardrum. It was a man's voice, a deep bass voice.

"AND YOU ARE ME!" the voice shouted.

His heart sank. Coren recognized the voice. Hevak. It was Hevak's voice, coming out of Lenora's mouth.

And Lenora had been dreaming about Hevak—dreams in which Hevak called her, invited her to come to him.

He couldn't still be alive somewhere, could he? Coren had *seen* Lenora get rid of Hevak. He'd seen Hevak disappear. But then, Coren himself had been made to disappear by Hevak. And he had kept on existing anyway, sort of, in a strange gray world. And hadn't Lenora said that she'd seen Hevak in a gray world in her dream?

Coren's heart began to race. He'd been so busy worrying about losing his powers and the destruction of his private room that he hadn't bothered to focus on Lenora and her dreams. And now he couldn't wake her. And he couldn't enter her mind or her dreams to find out what was happening there because he had no powers!

Yes, he thought grimly, it has all of the earmarks of Hevak.

"Lenora," he shouted. "Wake up! Please!" But nothing happened.

"Eee!" Leni shrieked. "I've sat in a puddle! My dress is ruined, completely and totally ruined!"

Leni, Coren thought. Of course! Leni had all of Lenora's powers. Leni could imagine, just for a couple of minutes, that he, Coren, had his powers back—the way Lenora did in that town out in the countryside, or when he'd overhead Mud's thoughts. And then Coren *could* enter Lenora's mind.

"Leni!" Coren exclaimed. "Come over here and help me. Something has happened to Lenora. She's fallen into a deep sleep and I can't wake her. I think she's under some kind of—"

"Spell?" Leni squealed, so excited that she crawled over to Coren, right through a large puddle, without even a single thought about her dress. "I know all about spells! When I was a little girl back home in Gepeth, I read a fantasy book where a princess falls asleep under a spell and guess what, Coren! Guess who's the *only* person that could wake her!"

Coren's patience was almost gone. "I have no idea," he said. "No idea at all."

"A prince! And you're a prince! You can do it! But"—she paused and blushed and giggled annoyingly—"you have to kiss her! That's the way you do it! By kissing her! Right on the mouth! Isn't that ever so sweet?"

Coren exploded. "This is *not* one of your fantasies, Leni. Lenora is fast asleep and I think something awful may be happening to her. I have to be able to enter her mind so I can find out what it is. Maybe she'll even be able to hear me once I get inside. But I don't have my powers. So *you* have to help me. Now!"

"Good heavens," Leni said, putting her hands on her hips. "Some people around here sure are awfully full of themselves. Remember, Mr. Pushy, I *am* helping you. I'm telling you how to wake her up. Kiss her."

"Don't be silly," Coren said. "This *is not* one of your stories."

"Then I'll do it!" Cori said, swaggering forward. "I'm a prince, too, after all!"

"Good idea, Cori," Leni said. "Don't you dare enjoy it, though, or else!"

"You will *not* kiss her," Coren declared. "If anyone is going to kiss her, it'll be me!"

"Good," Leni said. "I knew you'd come to your senses."

Feeling foolish, Coren bent over and gently kissed Lenora on the lips. Despite himself, he waited to see if she would wake up.

"I LOVE YOU!" Lenora shouted. Which would have been very reassuring, if she hadn't shouted it in Hevak's rich low voice.

"Good heavens," said Leni. "What's happened to her voice? She must be catching a cold."

Cold or not, Lenora kept right on sleeping.

"I told you," Coren said to Leni. "I said it wouldn't work."

But Leni was too busy staring down at Lenora to even hear him. "She's glowing," Leni said, her eyes wide.

Coren turned and looked.

"She *is* glowing!" he exclaimed. A sunny yellow light seemed to be emanating from Lenora—her entire body was surrounded by it.

"My," said Leni, "I wish I could do that. It creates quite an effect. Look how pretty it makes her look."

It did make her look pretty. Coren began to think of how wonderful she was, of how much he loved her and adored her. He wanted to simply sit there and worship her and bathe in her wonderful glow.

"AND YOU LOVE ME!" Hevak's voice shouted from out of the glow.

No! Coren shook his head violently back and forth, trying to clear his thoughts. Lenora was in trouble! He couldn't just sit there and let it happen.

"Yes, yes, I love you," Leni murmured.

"Love you, love you," Cori echoed.

Coren could see their happy faces radiant in the reflected glow that seemed to hold their eyes like a magnet.

"No!" he shouted, grabbing both of Leni's shoulders in a fierce grip and shaking her. "No! Stop it! Something strange is happening here! Something very strange. We have to wake her up! Please!"

As he shook, Leni's eyes changed. Now she was actually looking at him—and so was Cori.

"Unhand her, you brute!" Cori said.

As he spoke the glow diminished somewhat—and for a brief moment, Lenora's eyes opened a little, and she seemed to be looking at him.

But then they closed again.

"Leni," Coren said. "Please! It's an emergency, can't you see that? All you have to do is imagine that I have my powers back for a few minutes, so I can enter her thoughts. You have to help me get into her mind!"

"But Coren—the Balance! I can't do that, I just can't!"

The glow seemed to be getting stronger again, and larger. Leni had to help him, she just had to.

A thought suddenly occurred to him. "If I were you, Leni," he said in an ominous voice, "I'd be really worried."

"Me? Worried? Why?"

"Think about it. You and Lenora are so very alike. What happened to her in the past also happened to you, right? So, what's happening to her now—" He paused and stared down at Lenora's unconscious body. "Like I said," he continued, "if I were you, I'd be very, very worried.

For what seemed like a terribly long time, Leni just stood there, also staring down at Lenora.

"Okay," she finally said in a grim voice. "I'll do it."

"Oh, thank you, thank you!"

"Just don't you dare tell Agneth. I'll give you two minutes. Two minutes—no more and no less."

And suddenly, he could read Leni's thoughts.

Because it would be horrible, she was thinking, *just lying around and getting my makeup all smeared, and besides which, it couldn't be good for the Balance, me being in a trance like that, surely it couldn't. Who'd fix the smears? Who'd keep my darling Cori in line? Who'd remember to polish the napkin rings or set out the place cards for the evening meals? No question about it, I have to do it for the good of the Balance, I do, and that's that, and besides which—*

Coren had his powers back.

Quickly he refocused his attention, turned off Leni, and entered Lenora's mind.

Yes, he could hear her thoughts now—except they weren't

really thoughts, just feelings. Strong feelings of yearning and admiration. What was she finding so compelling?

He decided to do something he rarely did, move into her subconscious, go into her dream with her, so he could see what she was seeing.

And suddenly he was there.

CHAPTER 19

It is gray. Gray mists rise up all around her. She is wading through the gray as if it were water. She feels like it is water. She can hardly breathe. It is suffocating her.

At the back of her mind, something tickles. A memory. A boy. Red hair. And then it's gone. She is alone. No memories. She's not even sure who she is.

Then she hears a name being called. "Lenora! Lenora!" It sounds familiar. The name must be hers. Yes, that must be her name. Where is the sound coming from? She moves toward it.

The mist right in front of her begins to dissolve. A glow is penetrating the mist, a beautiful soft yellow glow. The glow is moving toward her. Someone is moving toward her, surrounded by a yellow glow.

It is he who calls her name. It is he. It is Hevak.

His voice is soft, melodious, golden, like honey or sweet syrup. He bursts through the mist, filling her world with bright golden light. He is resplendent. Tall, black hair, a gleaming smile, and eyes, glowing eyes so full of goodness, so full of compassion, so full of—

They're full of it, all right, thought Coren grimly, using all his force to wrench himself out of the vision. Now he was separate from Lenora again, watching her thoughts from a safe distance.

And things were even worse than he'd thought. That was Hevak in there, glowing away like some gigantic deformed glow worm inside Lenora's mind. It was so bright in there,

Coren had to look away—pull himself away.

But there was no question about it. Glow and all, it was still the same greasy hair, the same self-satisfied arrogant smile. It was still Hevak.

How *could* it be? Well, Lenora must have dreamed him up. He must have surfaced out of her subconscious somehow.

Which meant he could just go right back in there again! Hevak was no threat unless Lenora let him be one.

But then, why couldn't he wake Lenora up? Perhaps it was just the strength of her dream. As he watched, Lenora began to move toward Hevak. She was entering the glow that emerged from him, beginning now to shine in it herself.

This was bad. And Hevak looked so deceptively wonderful. He was exuding goodness and warmth. He was so loving, so kind, so full of—

It. Coren once more pulled himself back. It had been close maybe, but he knew Hevak better than to be fooled by a cheap trick like that—even if it *was* Lenora's subconscious doing it.

Something had to be done, and fast. He spoke to Lenora, mind to mind.

"Lenora! It's Coren!"

She stopped dead. She looked confused.

The glow now surrounding her brightened, became more intense.

"Never mind him, Lenora. He'll love us both soon. Come on, step into the love. Just a little closer."

"No!" Coren screamed into her mind. "No, Lenora!"

She looked startled.

"You have to wake up, Lenora. You have to!"

"Go away." It was Lenora's voice. Coren's heartbeat quickened. He was getting through to her. At least she was talking to him now.

"No, Lenora, I can't go away. You're in danger. Do you understand? Your body won't wake up. You've been sleeping far too long. Wake up now, Lenora. Now!"

He said the last words quite harshly. His tone was such a contrast to Hevak's that it seemed to be jarring her more than convincing her, but Coren would try anything at this point.

Lenora's eyes focused on the pest screaming behind her, interrupting her lovely feeling of peace. Red hair, freckles, puny but sweet. Who was that again?

"It's me, Lenora, Coren." Coren was thrilled. He could hear her thoughts. She had broken away from Hevak just for a second to wonder about him.

"Lenora, please. I'm your fiancé. We're about to be married. We love each other. And that over there is your enemy Hevak! Your enemy!"

Enemy? This redheaded boy was certainly foolish. She felt an intense and loving pity for him. Poor thing, to be so deluded, so very wrong, so very foolish. Hevak was her friend, not her enemy. He loved her, he glowed in the hugeness of his love for her. Why couldn't the poor foolish boy see that?

"I'm not foolish, Lenora," Coren thought back to her. "It's Hevak! He is dangerous, he is, he is! You have to wake up!"

He said the word Hevak with so much sincere loathing that Lenora was startled again. And then, suddenly, she knew who she was and she looked around. . . .

Coren was with her. And Hevak was facing her. But not the Hevak she remembered. A different Hevak, a—

It was like a door slamming shut. In a blink of an eye, Coren was gone.

"You idiot!" Coren exploded at Leni. "I'd just gotten through to her!"

"I said two minutes," Leni said. "The two minutes are up."

Coren bit back a retort. He didn't have time for Leni now. He bent over Lenora. He had to bring her back while she was "awake" in her dream. "Lenora! Lenora!"

For a brief instant, her eyelids flickered. But only for an instant. They closed again immediately, and her breathing changed, became deeper, more regular.

And now she was glowing again, brighter and brighter with every passing instant.

It was too late. She had turned back to Hevak, obviously, entered the glow again, and now it was shining right through her, as if she had somehow become a part of it, part of Hevak.

But it was impossible. Hevak was a figment of Lenora's imagination, part of her subconscious. She'd dredged Hevak up and made him good—to make herself feel better for creating something so bad, maybe. But whatever the reason, Hevak couldn't really be there. He couldn't, could he?

He had to be, Coren realized with a sinking feeling. A figment even of Lenora's powerful subconscious wouldn't have been able to make her fall asleep like that, totally against her will. Lenora's will was her strongest quality.

So it *was* Hevak. Not dead, not gone. He had survived somehow, he was somewhere and he wanted Lenora back. He wanted her to be one with him again, just the way he wanted it before.

No, Coren told himself as he looked down at Lenora's glowing face. Not the way he wanted it before. When Lenora was under Hevak's spell before she had become just like Hevak himself, evil, self-seeking. Now, her sleeping face exuded nothing but warmth and love.

And inside Lenora's thoughts, Hevak had looked like that, too. Totally good. As Coren watched the glow inch its way outward from Lenora's sleeping form, he found himself thinking that Hevak wasn't so bad after all, that he should take pity on him, forgive him, love him.

No. It was a trick. He would never forgive Hevak, never. And he would never trust him.

And yet, the more Lenora glowed—and she was glowing more all the time—the harder he was finding it to stick to his resolve.

Just then, Sayley burst into their room. "You'd better come fast! It's that awful boy Mud! He and a whole lot of those Skwoes are downstairs, and they say they're taking over the castle!"

CHAPTER 20

"Taking over the castle?" Coren repeated. "How could they? *Why* would they?"

"Mud says he met the others on the road on his way home—they were already most of the way here. It seems that after we left, they had a meeting and decided the situation in the castle was too dangerous for them. It's a change and they hate things changing. That's why they've come to take over the castle!"

"They won't take over *my* castle," said Cori, leaping to his feet and waving his broom-sword. I'll cut them all to ribbons first!"

"No, you won't," Coren snapped. "We don't need anyone being cut to ribbons!"

"Why not?" Sayley demanded. "They're disgusting. They're hardly human at all! They deserve to be cut to ribbons! Especially that Mud—he'd make wonderful ribbons. Golly— what's happened to Lenora?" Sayley was so excited that she hadn't until now, even noticed that Lenora was lying on the bed in an ever-enlarging pool of golden light.

Coren quickly told her what had happened.

"I bet *I* could wake her up," said Sayley. She closed her eyes and imagined Lenora awake. Nothing happened, except that the pool of light around Lenora grew even larger.

Sayley opened her eyes and shook her head. "Her will always was stronger than mine."

What a startling idea, Coren thought. *Could Sayley be right? Could Lenora's refusal to wake up be an act of her own will?*

Leni was kneeling by the bed and was now actually inside the expanding pool of light. Coren could see her gazing hypnotically at Lenora, a look of total devotion on her face.

"Leni!" Coren shouted. He reached into the glow, and, resisting the thoughts of passive loving acceptance that suddenly flooded his head, grabbed her by the hand and pulled her out.

"Unhand her, you brute!" said Cori, pointing the broomsword at Coren.

Coren just gave him a withering look. "Why don't you just dry up, big mouth?" he said. Cori was so flabbergasted at the timid Coren defying him that he actually lowered the broomsword.

"If I wasn't in an especially kind and loving and forgiving mood," said Leni, rubbing the spot on her arm where Coren had grabbed her, "I'd be really mad at you, Coren, for being so mean to my darling Cori. But I'm too nice right now to be mad, and I forgive you and I love you and I hope you feel the same."

"You love—? You hope I—?" Coren stared at Leni, herself now glowing a little, in disbelief. "Lenora's getting dangerous," he finally said. "Very dangerous. We're just going to have to stay away from her until we can figure out what to do about this mess. Let's get out of here and go down and see what those Skwoes are up to."

Sayley looked doubtful. "Will Lenora be all right if we leave her here all by herself?"

"Did you see what happened to Leni when she got near to Lenora? She actually thought about someone else other than herself! Leni! Oh no, Sayley, I think Lenora's going to be perfectly safe here—as safe as she's going to be as long as she's in this condition. And we're probably safer as far away from her as possible—until I can figure a way to snap her out of this."

"Well, then," said Sayley, "follow me. The real action's going on in the dining room."

What they saw as they headed down the stairs and through the corridors was shocking. There were Skwoes everywhere—hundreds of them, it seemed, all wearing exactly the same blue uniforms, cleaning with a vengeance, lifting some of the carpets and tacking others down, washing down walls, painting, hanging wallpaper, sweeping, cleaning, washing, dusting. The smells of soap and disinfectant filled the air.

At least, Coren thought, the castle will finally be spruced up a little.

But then he noticed something else. On the third floor landing, a group of Skwoes with a huge ladder was in the process of changing the bulbs in the chandelier that hung high over their heads. But the figure teetering at the top of the very shaky and precarious ladder and looking scared out of his wits was not in a blue uniform—not, in fact, a Skwoe at all. It was Squalnog, the Royal Master of Heraldry. An Andillan courtier, actually climbing a real ladder!

"You missed that one over there," one of the Skwoes shouted up to Squalnog. "Twelve points, that is. Lazy good-for-nothing Swellhead."

"They're all the same," another Skwoe agreed. "No-account bums."

Everywhere they went, now, they could see Andillan courtiers among the Skwoes. They were taking orders from the Skwoes, pushing brooms and mops, removing wallpaper, carrying big loads of garbage, looking horribly morose and dejected. And to make it worse, the Skwoes were constantly lecturing them about their dirty clothes, about the disgusting state of the castle, about what worthless creatures they were. It made Coren furious.

"You," a Skwoe said as they arrived at the bottom of the stairs in the front gallery. "All you lazy Swellheads there on the stairs! Don't think you can sneak off and get out of doing your fair share, because you can't. I have a whole wing full of toilets that need cleaning. Walk this way."

"If I walked that way," said Sayley tartly, observing the Skwoe's rather bowed legs, "I could carry a toilet between my knees."

"And just who do you think you are anyway," Cori added hotly, "telling *me* how to walk? I am Prince Cori the Brave, and *you*, sirrah, are toast!" He gestured menacingly toward the bow-legged Skwoe with his broom-sword.

"That's telling him, Cori," Leni said. "If he thinks that I, Princess Leni of Gepeth, am actually going to put my delicate royal hands into a toilet, of all places, well, he has another think coming!"

Coren could see a dark cloud pass over the face of the bow-legged Skwoe. Any minute now they were going to be gathered up by force and thrown into a dungeon. Or worse, actually sent off to do the toilets.

"Sayley," Coren hissed urgently. "Imagine we're all dressed in those Skwoe uniforms—right now! And change that stupid broom-sword of Cori's into a real broom."

She gave him a quizzical look—but Coren could feel the clothes shift on his body. He and Sayley and Cori and Leni were all dressed in blue.

"Good," he whispered. "And the rest of you just shut up—especially *you*, musclehead." He turned back to the bowlegged Skwoe. "Forgive me, sir," he said, "but we have instructions to head to subsector G53 of Section Y145 and, uh"—he remembered Cori's broom—"uh, sweep. Yes, that's it. Sweeping duty is our roster for this time frame. Musclehead Girth Y-even-bother-living has the broom, see? Delaying us will cost you many, many points. A kajillion, maybe, with five off for good behavior." Coren wasn't exactly sure he knew what he was talking about, and he hoped the Skwoe didn't either.

He didn't, apparently. He seemed so confused by their sudden change of costume that he stared blankly at them, jaw dropped.

Thank goodness, thought Coren as he gestured the others to follow him down the hall toward the dining room, that the Skwoes have so little imagination. The bowlegged fellow couldn't even begin to absorb the impossible thing that had just happened.

"This color is terrible on me," Leni whined as they rushed down the corridor past yet more working Skwoes. "It makes me look sallow, me, of all people! And I hate pants! Ladies don't wear pants, you know. The occasional pair of jodhpurs, maybe, while horse riding—but never just plain boring pants. Never inside. I must look awful!"

"If you're thinking about changing them back," Coren said, "don't—remember the toilet bowl. Stay the way you are and try to look unobtrusive."

"My Leni could never look unobtrusive," Cori said proudly. "She's much too magnificent! Even in those silly pants!"

"I told you they were silly!" wailed Leni. "I told you! I'll never live this down, never!"

The dining room was in total chaos.

Or rather, in total order—so much order that it was totally confusing.

There were Skwoes everywhere, and they seemed to be directing the operations throughout the castle. They stood at various places around the room, looking important and holding large stacks of papers. As other Skwoes rushed into the room to get instructions, they consulted their papers, checked items off, and then sent the others flying off to work again. The traffic through the door was never ceasing. Coren and the rest had to quickly scurry out of the path of Skwoes with their minds totally focused on duty or be knocked over.

Every few moments, one of the Skwoes checking off items would hand a sheet of paper to another Skwoe standing near him, who would rush with it toward the dining table and start bawling out the names of the checked-off tasks: "window replacement in corridor three, wing five" or "insulation removal, central attic."

At the table, still another group of Skwoes stood in a row in front of strange-looking square machines covered with buttons that they incessantly punched with their fingers. As they punched, they called out ever-increasing numbers of points— "Four hundred points!" "Five hundred and twenty points!" "Seven hundred and thirty-eight points!"—and another row of Skwoes standing behind them seemed to be recording these numbers in large black books. The room was filled with Skwoes working and shouting and moving back and forth.

At the center of it all, Coren could see, stood his parents, Lenora's parents, and Kaylor, the Thoughtwatcher. They were having a loud and, it seemed, very heated discussion with some Skwoes—who, as Coren approached, turned out to be familiar. It was the boy Mud and the old man who'd thrown them in prison—Sud Girth O60.

Coren threaded his way carefully through the army of Skwoes, who were so intent on their various tasks that they didn't even seem to notice him. The uniform probably helped. He approached the group in the center just in time to hear his mother ranting at Sud.

"You'll all have to leave this instant!" she shrieked. "You can't just march in here like this and take over! Exactly who do you think you are?"

Queen Savet, meanwhile, was staring angrily at Mud, who was still dressed in brown toweling. "I ought to turn them *all* into towels," she said.

"Towels aren't good enough for them," Rayden said. "They'd be much better as—oh, I don't know, as a great big bunch of nothing. I'm going to just think hard and think them totally out of existence"

"No, wait, don't!" Kaylor wailed. "You can't do that, you can't! We need them!"

"She's right," Milda said. "Where will we get food from if they don't exist?"

"Well, yes," Kaylor agreed, "there's that of course. But actually, I was thinking about the Equilibrium. If the Skwoes didn't exist, there'd be nothing to balance off our own imagining powers. Who knows what might happen then? The entire universe might become unhinged."

"If you ask me," said Sud, "it's becoming unhinged already. That's why we're here, to set things right again, to create order, order, order, order, ORDER!" As he repeated the word "order," his eyes became glazed.

So, too, did Mud's, who was now also murmuring, "Order, order, order, ORDER!"

Things were getting unhinged all right, thought Coren grimly. The Skwoes seemed to be getting stranger with every passing moment. Not only had they deserted their usual activities in the Skwoe town, despite their intense dislike of change, and marched on the castle—now they seemed to be getting even more obsessed with patterns and schedules and rituals than usual. The various Skwoes moving in and out of the room seemed to have marked out invisible paths—for Coren, standing at the center of it all was like standing in the middle of the works of a clock and watching the various wheels turn into and around each other. In fact, Sud and Mud seemed almost hypnotized by the idea of order, as if they'd completely lost consciousness of their individual selves and become mere unthinking cogs in the machine.

As Coren watched them chant, Mud's clothing shifted back to being the same blue material as all the others wore.

"Sayley," Coren whispered, turning to the girl who had followed him through the crowd and was standing behind him. "Did you do that?"

"No," she said. "I was actually imagining him as a cucumber in vinegar, but it didn't work."

He turned to Lenora's mother and father.

"Not me," said Savet.

"Or me," Rayden added.

"I think," said Kaylor, looking even more anxious, "he did it himself. The Skwoes are getting more and more unimaginative with every passing instant, now that our own powers aren't there to balance them. I suspect the boy is simply refusing to accept anything done by imagination—and by now his resistance is so strong that he's actually unmaking the reality Savet created when those clothes became toweling."

"That's terrible," Coren said. "It could mean the end of us all."

"It certainly could," Kaylor agreed, giving Coren an accusing look. "This is what comes of refusing to use the powers one was born with!"

"Terrible, terrible," King Arno agreed, turning to Coren. "What are we to do, my boy?"

"Fight!"

"Oh no, thought Coren. Not now! It was the musclehead, of course.

"Fight to the end!" Cori shouted as he made his way across the room, unceremoniously pushing Skwoes out of his way as he came, looking ridiculous in the blue outfit Sayley had imagined him into and brandishing his broom like the sword it once was.

"Father," he shouted, "*I* will protect you." He moved toward the still-chanting Sud, the broom slashing the air. "You, sirrah! Call off your men. Get out of here. Or I'll slice you up, myself."

Sud stopped chanting and seemed to come back into himself—and as soon as he did, so did Mud. They both looked rather confused about what had just happened to them, but they seemed at least to be paying attention to their surroundings.

Well, Coren told himself, the musclehead had accomplished something useful, for once. Although it was a good thing he had a broom and not a sword, or else Sud would have had a sizeable hole in his chest.

"Put that silly broom down," Coren ordered Cori. Cori immediately did. Coren wondered why. Was he too getting caught up in the Skwoe's urge for order?

Meanwhile, another change was occurring behind him.

"My dress!" Leni shrieked at the top of her voice. "It's back! I'm a lady again! And don't you start yelling at me, Coren, because I didn't do anything, nothing at all. It came back all by itself!"

So, too, at the same moment, had Coren's own clothing. Apparently, the unimagining emanating from Mud and Sud and the rest of the Skwoes was spreading. Now it had undone Sayley's wish that they all be in Skwoe uniforms.

If it kept on spreading, it would eventually get rid of Leni altogether—and the musclehead, too. They had been imagined into existence, after all, by Lenora. It might almost be worth waiting for it to happen.

But no, it wasn't—because now, Lenora's father's appearance was changing also. In the blink of an eye, King Rayden had become considerably shorter.

"Oh, dear," he said in a small voice. "I'm so embarrassed. I know it's against the Balance and all, but I was a mere lad when I imagined myself taller—a very short lad who already worshiped a much taller princess from afar and was afraid she would have nothing to do with someone so beneath her. Surely you understand, Savet darling?"

For a moment, the queen looked as if she were about to be very angry with him. Then, suddenly, she herself became a number of inches taller.

"Obviously, Rayden darling," she said in a small voice. "I do understand." She reached down and clasped his hand in hers.

"Listen," Coren said, turning to Sud. "This is a serious situation—you can see how serious it is. I believe we need some time, all of us, to think this through. I propose that you and your people return home, Sud Girth. *You* go home, and *we'll* promise not to make any more silly demands on you, and we'll all try to figure out a solution to the problem."

"No," Sud replied.

"No?"

"No. It's too late for that. Of course, we've known how you've been living all these years and we've turned a blind eye. But we can't anymore. You are like children. You can't take care of yourselves. We will have to get this place cleaned up and running properly. It's our responsibility to create order, order, order, order. We can't turn our back on you now—much as we'd like to."

"If you'd like to, just turn your backs on us," King Arno said. "We won't mind."

"Impossible," Sud declared. "And we have people going to all your villages and towns, too. Everyone is going to shape up. It's taking *valuable* time away from our work, but there's no choice. We can no longer live in the midst of this chaos and pretend it isn't. We must have order, order, order, order."

"Order, order, order, order," Mud repeated mindlessly.

Oh no, thought Coren, the imbalance is getting even worse. Now Skwoes all around him were picking up the chant. "Order, order, order, order!"

Soon all the work in the room had come to a standstill as the Skwoes joined the chant and their eyes became glazed. Then, their eyes still apparently unseeing, they began to move. The Andillans and Gepethians scrambled to get out of the way as the Skwoes around them moved mindlessly into a strange formation, paying no attention whatsoever to any obstacle in their path.

In a few moments, the Skwoes stood stiffly back to back in tight little groups of four, each of the four pointing outward in a different direction, and the groups had arranged themselves so that each of them was equidistant from the others. They looked as if they were taking part in some kind of strange life-size board game—as if they had just stopped being human beings with individual minds and wills all together.

As Coren and the rest tried to get out of the way of the formation that had developed right where they had been standing, they bumped into another one of these groups of four, which moved back out of the way, never missing a beat of the continuing chant. Eerily, all the other groups moved at almost exactly the same time, so that the groups remained equidistant from each other. And through it all, the chanting continued:

WE ARE UD! UD IRTH!
BUD NO MORE,
CUD NO MORE,
DUD NO MORE,
MUD NO MORE.
ZIRTH NO MORE,
VIRTH NO MORE,
TIRTH NO MORE,
GIRTH NO MORE.
WE ARE UD! CALL US UD! CALL US IRTH!

For a brief instant, the chanting ceased. The Skwoes took one step sideways to the right, then one step back. They were yet once more in the same formation, but now each was facing in a different direction. They started to chant again:

THE RULES OF ORDER!
RULE ONE, SECTION ONE, SUBSECTION ONE:
A WORLD WITHOUT ORDER IS A WORLD WITHOUT POINT.
RULE ONE, SECTION ONE, SUBSECTION TWO:
IMAGINATION IS POINTLESS.

"Imagination," said Leni, "is pointless." Now her eyes were glazing over also.

"Pointless," Queen Savet added. She grew even a little taller.

This is awful, Coren thought, panicking. Imagination is disappearing altogether! Everyone has gone berserk—and there's nothing I can do about it. There's nothing that anyone can do about it!

Then, all at once, the chanting stopped. The Skwoes and

everyone else turned toward the door, including Coren. As they did so, their faces were suffused with a warm glow, which poured through the door and completely filled the room.

As everyone watched in uncomprehending awe, the light got more and more intense. And now, a figure stood in the middle of it, in the doorway. It was a girl, a beautiful blond-haired girl.

It was Lenora.

Lenora had awakened.

CHAPTER 21

Everyone in the room stood there, bathed in the golden glow that now filled the room, and gazed at Lenora, adoring her. As they did so, the mood in the room shifted, so that they all seemed to be glowing inside as well as out.

I love her, Coren found himself thinking. I love Lenora. But not impurely as I did before, poor benighted fool that I was. Not as a fiancée, not as my future wife. I could never marry her, never. She is so good, so kind, so perfect, and I am just mere worthless dust under her perfect feet. How could I imagine a disgusting little nothing like me being married to the wonder of her in all her perfect and glorious wonderfulness? No, never. I love her. I adore her. I will devote my life to worshiping her from afar.

And Coren could sense that he was not alone, that everyone in the room felt as he did. As the glow suffused them, they had stopped worrying about their petty problems, about the end of imagination and the destruction of the Balance and the extinction of the entire world as they had always known it. How could such puny insignificant concerns matter at all, in the presence of the magnificent wonderfulness of Lenora? They couldn't. They didn't. Everyone adored her, loved her, planned to spend the rest of their lives worshiping her. And so they should.

"I love you," Mud murmured.

"Love you," Sud and Queen Savet echoed.

"Love you," everyone in the room repeated.

"Love you," Coren himself added, staring adoringly along with the rest of them into the perfect and perfectly loving face at the center of the golden glow.

As he gazed into it, he could sense a change in the face, in the eyes. They looked soulfully into the room, regarding everyone with infinite love, infinite pity. And there were tears in them. Lenora was displeased—displeased with them all. Displeased with him.

It was almost unbearable. He wanted her love, her concern, her compassion. Without it, he would have no choice but to wither up and die. How could he regain his good grace in the magnificent Lenora's tremendously wonderful eyes? How could he please her once more?

Her eyes, her expressive weeping eyes, told him. It was his love she wanted—but not for her, not for Lenora herself. She was too perfect for that, too complete to need his love. She wanted him to love mankind, to love the world, to love each and every living thing.

He did. He loved them all. He looked fondly around the room, at his mother, his father, his future in-laws. They were kind, wonderful people. How could he not love them? And Kaylor—the Thoughtwatcher had been mean and nasty to him for his own good, because she cared for him. He loved her, too. And there was Sud Girth, who was standing in front of him, and who was now embracing Queen Milda. Such a noble old gentleman, Coren thought. So full of good down-to-earth common sense. I love him. And Mud, too, he thought, his gaze shifting a little to take in the boy. Still a child, but with his head planted firmly on his shoulders, and with an amazing fortune in points for one so young. How could you help but love him? Why, even as he watched, Sayley had come over and taken Mud's hand in hers and was telling him what a great and wise people the Skwoes were and how truly loveable Mud himself was. He was. Coren agreed—he was a truly loveable boy.

And now Coren felt himself being embraced, by an arm thrown energetically around his shoulders.

"My closest and dearest friend," a voice boomed in his ear. "My comrade in arms! Prince Coren, I love you and I totally admire your spineless weakness, and you can be the biggest coward on earth if you want to be because I will always be here by your side to defend you!"

It was that musclehead Cori. Coren sensed himself pulling back—and at the same time, sensed Lenora's disapproval of him. He should not be rejecting the love of this fellow human—it was not loving. It was not nice.

I love him, Coren told himself. I do love Cori, I really do lo—.

And then, he realized what he was doing.

I really don't, he thought. I really can't stand the brainless idiot. He reached up and grabbed Cori's hand and flung the arm off his back, saying, "Go away, muscle boy."

Cori, startled, stared at him uncomprehendingly, as if he couldn't imagine someone not accepting his love. But then his gaze shifted, and in the next instant he had joined Mud and Sayley, and the three of them were joyfully hugging each other.

And Coren, who now knew for sure that the wonderful perfect Lenora was disappointed in him, felt an almost irresistible urge to join them.

This is awful, he told himself, resisting the urge. I have to get out of here. Right now, before it's too late.

He began to make his way out of the room, passing clumps of Skwoes offering each other all of their entire fortune of points just because they were so loveable, and meanwhile, becoming ever more intermeshed in complex group hugs. The closer he got to the doorway and Lenora, the stronger the glow became, and the harder he was finding it to resist loving everyone in the vicinity.

In fact, he now told himself, what was the point of resisting at all? It was silly of him, silly self-centered foolishness. Because he did love them all, did love the Skwoes, did love the trees and the thistles and each and every living thing on the face of the globe.

And Lenora approved. He knew she approved. He stood now right before her in the doorway, the warmth of her glow shining so strongly upon him that the heat was almost unbearable.

I will be burned, he thought, or blinded. My eyes are going black, I can feel my vision go. But it doesn't matter, because I love everyone.

Even as he thought these thoughts, he could feel the heat diminish, and his eyes began to see once more, and he knew that he could gaze on Lenora for as long as he wanted without danger to himself, that Lenora had sensed his need to bask in her glow and felt his love and granted him his desire.

And then, suddenly, the glow emanating from Lenora wavered, dimmed a little, and Coren found himself wondering where he was and what he was doing.

"Make way, make way," a strangely happy voice called out. "Make way for the happy hopper!"

It was Agneth, the Keeper, who had bumped into Lenora from the rear. Now he pushed her aside and entered the room. Agneth was hopping on one leg. He was still, it seemed, in the midst of some kind of mental breakdown, driven right out of his balance-loving mind by the recent imbalanced events.

"Happy hopping," he sang, hopping merrily around the

groups of hugging Skwoes. "Happy hopping, never stopping, that's the way, to hop today, hop, hop, hop!" He was so far out of his senses, it seemed, that he was quite impervious to the glow of love that once again began to flow from Lenora.

Which was, Coren realized, a good thing for himself. Because the momentary interruption had been enough to pull him back, remind him of his need to get away. The love had returned, pulling him in the other direction, creating an intensely painful tug of war in his mind. But he found he could pull back now, resist. He found he could actually walk around Lenora and the most intense part of her glow and through the door and out of the room, out of the wonderful presence, away from the joyful and perfect love he wanted and needed and resisted with all his might.

Out in the corridor, the glow was less strong, the need to return easier to resist. But it was still there. Coren could feel it in himself, in the intense sense of loss that filled him, and he could see it in the Skwoes working around him.

"That ladder is too heavy for you, Ud Irth," said one. "Let me carry it."

"No, Ud Irth, you've been working much harder than me, let me carry it."

"No, me."

"No, me."

"No," said a third Skwoe who had approached from the direction of the main hallway, "Let me carry the ladder and the two of you also, Ud and Ud. I know I'll be strong enough because I want to be, and if I really and truly want to be, then love will find a way."

Coren found himself thinking that he himself might carry the ladder and all three Skwoes, who so completely and surely deserved his compassion for their devotion to duty and each other. All he had to do was invite them to stand on the ladder and then he'd just pick it up and balance it on top of his head.

No, no, no. There was obviously no choice for Coren but to get completely and totally out of the castle and as far away from Lenora as he could.

CHAPTER 22

Coren sat under a tree, on the outskirts of a decaying and deserted village some distance from the castle. He'd had to come all this way before his mind completely cleared of kind thoughts and warm intentions. Or at least, almost completely— he was still feeling a surprising amount of compassion for the flies that buzzed so annoyingly around his head. The poor little things couldn't help it if he smelled so good to them. Except for that wave of water that had poured out of his room when he opened the door earlier, he hadn't bathed since the time he'd spent with all that decaying refuse in the Skwoe town.

Now that his mind was fairly clear, he could do some hard thinking. There had to be some way out of this mess.

If there was, he realized with a sinking feeling, he was obviously going to have to find it all by himself. The only person beside himself who wasn't mesmerized by Lenora's glow was Agneth—and Agneth was too busy hopping and singing to be of any help to anybody.

There had to be some way to get them all unmesmerized again. There had to be some way to get Agneth to stop hopping. Most of all, there had to be some way to get Lenora to stop glowing. All he had to do was figure out what that way was.

One thing seemed fairly certain. Going out to the Skwoe town had been a bad idea, since it had led to the Skwoes coming back to the castle—and the Skwoes coming into the castle had made things worse, much worse. The Andillan Balance had always depended on the two different peoples of the country living their lives opposite to and separate from each other.

But just as obviously, the whole mess hadn't been started by the Skwoes—or, for that matter, by any of the court Andillans. It was Coren's people losing their powers that had led to the Skwoes being discovered and coming to the castle and becoming so imbalanced. And he still had no idea why those powers had been lost in the first place.

He had his suspicions, though. Ever since he'd spent those few moments inside Lenora's thoughts, he knew he'd been wrong about those dreams she'd been having. They weren't just normal nightmares. Coren and his people had lost their powers just when those dreams began—and then, Lenora had been desperate to head out to the countryside for no obvious reason. It was almost as if she were being driven, forced to discover the Skwoes and lead them to the castle.

And it had something to do with Hevak. Hevak was there inside her thoughts. He'd been calling her to him. And then she'd begun to glow.

She must have gone to Hevak. Going to him had made her glow. And the glowing had caused everything else.

But why? Why was she glowing, and what did it have to do with Hevak?

If only his own powers weren't gone. If only he could enter her thoughts again and find out what was happening there. He loved Lenora so much, so very much. He couldn't stand being separated from her. He couldn't stand simply being one of multitudes she loved. If only he could see into her mind. If only he had his power back, even for a brief instant.

For a brief instant, he thought that he did—but then, immediately, it was gone again. He had only been imagining it, wishing so hard he almost believed it to be true.

But wait a minute! Earlier, when he'd been bathed in the glow, he'd wished for things and they actually seemed to happen. In fact, that seemed to be the main effect of Lenora's huge new love for everybody. She loved them so much, and so much wanted them to love each other, she gave them what they wanted and needed in order to express their love.

Well, he certainly loved Lenora—the old Lenora, but Lenora nevertheless. He wanted and needed her back the way she was. Maybe he could just go back into the castle and tell her that. Wouldn't her vast compassion feel his need and grant his desire and make her stop glowing and become his own Lenora again?

Probably not. For one thing, she loved everybody now, not just him. She'd take pity on him, certainly—but she'd never desert everybody else's needs just to satisfy his. That was the whole trouble with her now—she was too nice, too generous. It was very annoying.

And for another thing, by the time he entered the glow and got close enough to Lenora to talk to her, he'd probably be mesmerized again, loving everybody again. He'd probably end up asking her to make him into a towel so Lenora's mother could get in some folding time or into a target for that musclehead Cori to shoot arrows at or into a hunk of decaying meat for the flies to enjoy.

But if he just entered the edge of the glow—far enough in for Lenora to sense his need, close enough to the edge to keep his own will more or less intact—he might be able to get her to let him read her thoughts. And if he knew what was happening in there, maybe he could get right back out again and then figure out a way to stop it from happening. Yes, it just might work.

It was some hours later before Coren actually reentered the

glow. In the meantime, he'd taken a few precautions. First of all, he'd gone into one the deserted houses in the village and got some equipment. He'd found some old honey at the bottom of a jar and spread it on his arms and on his face. The result was just as he'd hoped—hundreds of flies had landed on him, and some ants had actually climbed onto his feet and moved upward over his legs, seeking out the honey. He was covered with bugs. It was exceedingly aggravating, exceedingly distracting—which was just what he wanted. With all those insects on him, it'd be hard to devote his whole attention to anything—even Lenora's total devotion.

He also found a long roll of rope. When he got fairly close to the glow—which had spread by now some distance out from the castle and bathed a wide swath of the surrounding coun-tryside—he tied one end of the rope to a tree and the other end to himself. Once he entered the glow he knew he would feel compelled to get closer and closer to its source. The rope would hold him back—long enough, he hoped, so that he could get safely out of there.

His heart beating fast, he walked toward the glow, swatting at flies and ants. It was for Lenora, he reminded himself—he had to do this, for Lenora. And then, trying to focus on how much he loved her and needed to know her thoughts, he stepped into the golden light.

The next step was into a memory—Lenora's memory. She must have sensed his need, because now he was seeing exactly what he wanted to know. He had entered the part of her mind where she stored her recollections of her recent experiences with Hevak.

She was walking in a gray mist. She couldn't remember who she was. But hadn't she been here before? It all looked so familiar.

Oh, now she remembered. She'd been having a strange dream about being a princess and about some odd people with no imagination. She laughed. It had been so silly. What had they been called? Skwoes! Dreams were so fantastical, weren't they?

In the dream, there was a redheaded boy she was engaged to. As if she'd ever become engaged to such a comical-looking fellow. And there were two of each of them—another Lenora, another redheaded boy. That was typical of dreams, though. They rarely make any sense.

She was happy to be back. Out of that ridiculous dream, back in the only reality there was.

The gray mist switched around her, and she knew that soon Hevak would come and find her. They were to meet, weren't they? Yes. They had great things to accomplish together. Great things.

And there he was! Tall, strong, handsome, exuding goodness and well-being. She was filled with joy as she rushed forward to meet him.

No, wait. There was something wrong, something scratching at the back of her mind, something behind her. She turned to look.

Why, it was that funny-looking boy from her dream! How did he get here?

He was trying to pull her back, trying to get her to stay away from Hevak.

"Lenora, don't do this. Think. I am Prince Coren. You are the Princess Lenora. This is a dream."

Silly boy. But it was hard to be annoyed with him—he was so human, so little, so deserving of compassion.

And now, suddenly he was gone. She sighed, then turned her attention back to Hevak again.

Hevak spoke. "He's right, Lenora. And you're right and I'm right."

Now here, Lenora thought, is someone who is obviously telling the truth. "How?" she asked.

"He's right. What you remember isn't a dream. You do live in that world. And you're right. This isn't a dream either. And I'm right because I tell you that the old evil Hevak is gone and replaced by a new Hevak dedicated to doing only good in the world. There will be no more war, Lenora, no more rivalry or bickering or even petty squabbles. Love will rule all, love, love!"

Love, she thought. Of course. Love is all we need.

"But," Hevak continued, "I can't come back without you, Lenora. I need you. I love you."

"I love you, too. But—I thought you were gone, gone forever. What happened to you? Where have you been, my beloved Hevak?"

"In another world. You did it, my beloved Lenora. You pushed me out of this world with such strength and such conviction that I went right through the nothingness and emerged on the other side. There is another world there, Lenora—a world completely reversed from this one. In that place I, too, was reversed. Since I had been all bad in your world, I became all good in this new one."

Yes, he was—all good. Lenora could sense his goodness.

"And I've used my goodness, Lenora—made all things good here, just as I made all things bad there. Here, now, the once angry lambs peacefully share enclosures with the meek lions, and the strong handsome women do half of the boring household tasks and allow the men to run some of their businesses and compete in their wrestling matches. The sophisticated country folk no longer look down on the unlearned and unmannerly city dwellers, and the city dwellers help the country folk to design their art installations and even write their poetry. The grass is always fresh and sparking sapphire blue, and the sky remains a beautiful clear green all day. There is not one little smidgen of badness left, here in my new world. It is perfect here now."

It sounded wonderful. It sounded good.

"It is, oh, it is, it surely is. But"—Hevak's voice became sad now—"But now, Lenora, now that I have made this world totally good, there is nothing left for me to do, no way for me to express my complete and total goodness. I need to act, need to be good, or I will wither away, cease to be."

No, no, never that. Not her beloved Hevak!

He gazed down at her beseechingly. She could feel the warmth of the gaze, see its golden glow. "It's time for me to spread my goodness to your world, Lenora. But you have to help me. You have to be good. You have to bring me back."

Yes!

"Yes! You and me, Lenora! Together, making a perfect world! You dreamed of it once. This time, it can happen."

"It can happen!" she shouted joyfully. "It can be good, oh so good!. We can be joined together—"

Yes! They were joined. She was one. She was love. Nothing but love, complete and perfect love.

She could feel the love emerging from her, bathing all. They needed her, needed her love. She would give them what they needed.

She moved through her people, loving them, loving their love of each other, sensing their needs, fulfilling their wishes. It was hard work, ever so hard. So many to love, so many needs, so many wishes to fulfill. But she was love, perfect love, she would do it, she would.

This one, this redheaded boy inside her head, inside her thoughts. He loved her. She had granted his wish to know her mind, but now, she sensed, he needed to leave, to flee her love. She was good. It was hard, so hard. But she would grant all wishes. She would grant his wish.

Coren felt a wrenching snap as Lenora pushed him out of her thoughts, just in time.

CHAPTER 23

Grimly, Coren grabbed onto the rope and began to pull himself back along it, out of the glow, out of Lenora's perfect love. One instant longer in there and he'd be gone, sunk into goodness like everybody else.

By the time he made it back to the tree he'd tied the rope to, he was only a short distance away from the edge of the golden light. It seemed to be growing more quickly all the time. Something had to be done.

Unfortunately, Coren had no idea what it could be. Still, he told himself as he swatted at flies and ants and tried unsuccessfully to rub the honey off his face, at least I know what's happened.

Lenora was with Hevak now, one with him now. Hevak had invaded her, was controlling her, was using her—that glow was his. He was planning to take over the world, just as he had before. This time, he claimed to be good, and he claimed to be taking over the world for good reasons, not evil ones. But he was Hevak still—he couldn't be good, it simply wasn't possible. Was it?

And even if it was, what Hevak had done to Lenora couldn't be good. What he was planning for the world couldn't be good. Could it?

Coren thought about it as he untied the rope from the tree. You couldn't just make everything and everybody good. For one thing, what would happen to the Balance then? Without evil to balance off the good, would good still be good? How could you choose to be good if you couldn't also choose to be bad? Didn't you need evil to understand what good was? Would a world without any evil and without any possibility of evil actually be a good place?

I know one thing for sure, Coren thought. It would be a very boring place. People being good all the time, doing what they ought to, not causing fusses or getting into trouble.

It was exactly the world Coren had dreamed of before he met Lenora. It was hard to admit it, but now, he knew, he'd hate it.

And how strange, how very strange, that it should be created by Lenora, of all people—Lenora, who hated boredom above all else.

But that Lenora was gone now, devoured by Hevak's goodness—just as everybody else was being devoured by Hevak's goodness.

Devoured. A new thought struck him. Hevak's powers had grown as the powers of others had waned, as Coren himself and the other Andillans lost their mental abilities, and as the Gepethian's imaginations had begun to work so erratically. It was, indeed, just as if Hevak had devoured their powers, absorbed them into himself, used them to enter and fill Lenora thoughts and then the world. Was that why she'd begun to want to imagine a perfectly good world? Or was it her wish to imagine that world that had beckoned Hevak back again?

It didn't matter. Hevak was Lenora's creation in the first place. It all came back to Lenora. It always came back to Lenora.

But understanding that certainly wasn't going to help Coren to solve the problem. Hevak and Lenora had all the strength and held all the cards. Coren himself had no powers to use, and neither did anybody else. Any hour now, of course, more wedding guests would be arriving, guests from different places with different sorts of power. The Grafnidians might be able to defy Hevak with their superstrength; the Minannians might calm him with their powerfully soothing music. Or the Plasmanoids might use their remarkable skills of elasticity to stand outside the dangerous glow, reach inside, and constrain him with their hands.

For that matter, the Kitznoldians might just plant fast-growing vines all around him and choke him to death.

But Hevak was probably too strong for them all now—they'd be sure to lose the powers before they had a chance to use them.

It was hopeless, utterly hopeless. Coren leaned against the tree, so engrossed in his thoughts that he didn't even notice the tendrils of golden light that had been advancing resolutely toward him and that were now dancing delicately around his ankles.

He had to think—and it was so hard to keep your thoughts straight with all these ants crawling all over you and all these endless pesky flies.

I wish, he thought angrily, that all these bugs would just go away. And also, all the honey.

The bugs were gone. The honey was gone.

But Coren didn't even notice. He was gone, too, gone into a hypnotic trance as the glowing light arose around him.

I love, he thought. I love each and all. I need to express my love.

He rose to his feet, and staring unseeingly in front of him, walked implacably into the glow and back toward the castle.

CHAPTER 24

They are my people, Lenora thought, looking around the dining room with her heart aglow. They are so frail, so completely and totally flawed and inconsequential compared to me and my perfect love. And yet still they try, they try so hard to love, to care, to be compassionate, to step beyond the undeniably narrow boundaries of their shallow little selves. It's so courageous of them. It's so sweet.

They need my love. They need my help. They need, they need so much, so very much.

That one over there, for instance, that pale and merely human imitation of the divine Lenora herself. Leni, she was called, poor little mortal. Leni needed now, desperately needed.

My hair, Lenora could hear her thinking. All this hugging and loving everybody has completely ruined it. It is quite out of control!

Smiling compassionately, Lenora reached out and began to arrange the doll-like little human's hair, intuitively understanding the style that would please her. She quickly wound Leni's long blond tresses around a slim deep green ribbon until an intricate design, piled on top of her head, emerged.

"Oh, wondrous Lenora, thank you, thank you," Leni said as Lenora held up the mirror she had just created so that Leni could survey the results. "It's just perfect—just as perfect as you are yourself. I love it—not for myself of course, because I'm not thinking about myself, I wouldn't do that, not ever. No, I love it because looking at it and admiring it will make others so happy." Then her smile dimmed a little. "Although it does make this old dress look just a little, well, tacky."

Sighing in the depths of her infinite pity, Lenora changed Leni's dress into the concoction of pure spun gold that she could see Leni picturing inside her mind.

"Oh yes, yes, yes!" exclaimed Leni, posing in front of the mirror. "Magnificent! It will give so much pleasure to so very, very many. It's a little tight under the arms, perhaps."

Loosening the arms, Lenora simultaneously widened the focus of her attention and felt the deep love, and the deep need, of a number of the others gathered around her.

As she did so, Prince Cori the Brave found his broom finally replaced with a sword, a large curved one with a serrated titanium edge and a Snetzerland flesh-entering finish. He himself was standing in the most magnificent suit of armor any of them had ever seen. It was gold with silver-plate accents, and a jeweled hilt for the sword hung at his belt.

"Oh, Cori!" sighed Leni, managing for a brief instant to pull her gaze away from her own image in the mirror. "You look magnificent. How kind of you."

"You look magnificent, too, my little dove," Cori answered.

"Yes, I do, don't I? I'm so pleased for you all! The shoes don't quite match, of course." Even as she said it, the shoes did match.

In the same moment, a large green dragon's head thrust itself through the doorway and peered into the room, the flames emerging from its nostrils slightly scorching some of the Skwoes who stood nearby.

"A savage dragon threatening our very lives!" Cori shouted gleefully. "Just what I wanted! Now I can single-handedly save you all and show my deep, deep love and concern! At it, at it, at it!" Brandishing the sword and nearly amputating a number of human limbs, he clanked his way across the room toward the dragon.

Cori's clumsy but dangerous flight through the gathered crowd was hardly even noticed, as Lenora sensed and fulfilled the needs of more and more of her people.

"Oh, thank you for giving me my powers back," said Queen Milda inside Lenora's mind.

"And me," added Arno.

"And me and me and me." The words echoed in Lenora's minds as hundreds of Andillans inside the palace and out joined the mental conversation. As she proceeded with her work, Lenora could hear the conversation continuing at the back of her mind, as various Andillans entered each others thoughts and found hidden desires and competed with each other to fulfill them.

Meanwhile, Lenora's father was admiring a shiny new hunting bow, which meant that he could provide nutritious food for others at no cost. And her mother was standing by the table in delighted awe.

"The perfect wedding banquet," she exclaimed. "Just what I'd been imagining!"

The long table was truly magnificent. Tapers burned down its center, held in gold candlesticks; in front of each place was an individual bouquet of fresh flowers; gold covers sat over gold plates and cutlery, steam escaping, bringing with it exotic smells. A perfectly folded linen napkin lay beside every plate.

"The guests will be so pleased," Savet said. "I only hope they won't think I'm trying to impress them, because I'm not, of course, I'm doing it all for them. I just want them to have a good time."

Divining her mother's loving concern, Lenora removed

some of the candles from the candlesticks and some of the flowers from the bouquets.

"Yes, that'll make them feel more comfortable," Savet said. "Much less ostentatious. But perhaps silver would be better than gold? Or just some fancy china?"

As she spoke, the table shifted in front of her eyes. In a few moments, there was nothing there but a bare uncovered table with one dry piece of bread and a glass of water at every setting. There weren't even any napkins.

"Perfect,"Savet said. "Nobody could be made to feel envious about that. Of course, it's not terribly nutritious."

The pieces of bread turned into enriched whole-grain muffins. Indeed, the table kept shifting again and again as Lenora continued to go about her work with others and Savet kept changing her mind about what would make her wedding guests happiest.

"I'm starved!" Sayley exclaimed as the most fancy of the banquets reappeared. She immediately plunked herself down at one of the gold plates and began to eat—and was most upset when the slice of roast beef she was munching on turned into fried liver and onions. Sayley hated fried liver, especially with onions. Lenora quickly turned it back into beef and also made Sayley and her plate invisible to Savet, who would not be at all happy about part of her perfect wedding banquet being eaten in advance. Then Lenora turned Mud into an actual bog of mud, which lay sloppily under Sayley's feet as she sat at the table. Sayley happily paddled her invisible bare feet in the cool and delightfully squishy muck as she devoured her delicious beef.

Mud had wished for his new state. Puddles are not expected to have an imagination or even to think very much at all. And as long as he was lying there being damp and dirty and giving pleasure to others as was his duty, it wasn't costing him a single point. He might even be getting quite a few.

Lenora left him as a puddle and awarded him a hundred and twenty-seven points. She also topped up the points' accounts of all the other Skwoes in the room, who simultaneously told each other that the good thing about being rich was the opportunity it gave you to be of assistance to others, and who then immediately began to offer the points to each other absolutely free, no strings attached, for the benefit of humankind.

Lenora could see that the world around her was filling up with goodness.

And the goodness was spreading. Even as she dealt with the needs of those in the room with her, she could sense others farther away, loving, caring, needing. They, too, now basked in the glow of her compassion. They, too, needed her help and her pity.

Out there, for instance, outside the castle, a boy, a red-headed boy, was leaning against a tree. It was Coren. Once upon a time, back when she had been small-minded enough to be selective in her love, she had chosen him out of the pitiful throngs and actually cared for him more than any of the others. How silly she was, then, how narrow. But Coren, too, needed her, wanted her love. She encouraged him to come toward her and fulfill his need.

And all the while, she fulfilled the desires of her loving people and made the world a better place.

The Andillans were vociferous in their huge urge to think up better realities for their friends and neighbors. Lenora had to concentrate hard and slow down their imaginations, lest the blinding pace of their changing visions unsettle and bedazzle them all. It would also give them more time to praise her for her loving kindness to them. Not that she actually needed any praise, of course—but it certainly showed their ferocious and wonderful urge to be good. How sweet they were, how very sweet.

Meanwhile, the Skwoes everywhere in the land begged Lenora to think up new machines—so she created machines to clean the floor, machines to clean the carpets, machines to clean the walls, machines to clean their clothes, machines to fix and make clothes, machines to help them add all their numbers in their books ever more rapidly, machines to help them sell their materials, machines for harvesting their crops and for fixing their streets and for pruning their trees. They were very noisy machines, and they made the work go very fast—faster and faster all the time, in fact, as the Skwoes became quickly dissatisfied with the machines, she had to imagine better ones for the sake of efficiency and the good of people everywhere. She imagined improvements so quickly that the Skwoes hardly had begun to thank her for them before they became dissatisfied and demanded even better ones from her.

But then, what could you expect of mere fallible humans?

It was hard, so very hard, all this endless fulfilling of needs, but Lenora never flagged. Her mind raced from room to room, corridor to corridor, village to village, town to town, finding and fulfilling needs at an ever-quickening pace.

And even as Lenora sensed the neediness of her people and fulfilled their wishes, the needs changed. They were becoming ever more pressing, more demanding. Keeping up with it all took constant attention, eternal vigilance. It was very tiring. It was even a little annoying—or would have been, had she not been too good and too perfect to ever feel annoyance.

But it had to be done. They were so fragile, so frail. They were trying so hard. They deserved all the pity she could give them, even if it took every single minute of her precious time and all her precious stores of goodness.

But why couldn't they be content for once?

Here, for instance, was that annoying Leni again, niggling at Lenora's thoughts, feeling the need for yet another change in her appearance. She wanted her hair to actually move. Lenora made it happen. The hair on Leni's head changed constantly, one moment up in a fantastic intricate design, the next pulled back simply off her face, the next swept to the side, the next swept to the other side.

"It's a new hairdo every minute!" Leni exulted as she stared into the special top-quality hand mirror she had also needed so very much. "What a thrill for everybody! Oh, thank you, miraculous Lenora who loves us all! Could you do the same for my dress?"

Who does she think I am? Lenora found herself thinking. I can only do so much at once! She altered the dress according to Leni's wishes and was surprised to find herself exasperated at how quickly Leni ran away from her to show the others, after only two or three brief words of adulation and praise for the miraculous gift. Frail and fickle. Typically human.

But there was no time to think of that. A Skwoe in the Skwoe town Number Three, Sector 5, Subsector 4G, had come up with an idea for a machine that made other machines.

And Kaylor, the Thoughtwatcher, was having a hard time keeping up with all the imbalanced thoughts of the Andillans and was in need of thoughtwatching assistance.

And a crew of Skwoes in the west wing of the castle had totally cleaned and painted and spruced up all the rooms there, and they yearned desperately to have the place dilapidated and dirty yet once more, so that they wouldn't have to stop cleaning and organizing and helping others to be just as clean and efficient and good as they were themselves. It was the third time, Lenora realized, that she had had to undo all their work for them.

Meanwhile, Queen Milda was feeling the need for a real dragon flambé made from the flesh of a real dragon—not out of self-centered gluttony, of course, but merely to calm her stomach and therefore make her more loving and loveable to others. Lenora made the flambé from the remains of a dragon Prince Cori had defeated in noble and particularly bloody battle for the good of all and then insisted on dragging back to the castle to show everybody. Cori himself was out in the courtyard now, fighting the two-headed dragon he'd hoped for to replace it.

Sayley was enjoying her roast beef dinner so much, and thinking about how happy the cooks would be that she was enjoying it, that she was hoping never to feel full. So she continued to sit at the table and stuff her mouth, every once in a while patting her increasingly round and increasingly huge stomach. She was getting a little tired of beef, though. Wouldn't the world be a better place if it was liver instead, and if she actually did like liver.

Lenora immediately made the beef into liver, but for some reason she didn't quite understand, waited just a few short moments before it became true that Sayley actually liked it. Let her suffer a little, Lenora found herself thinking. Let her know what it's like to be me.

Children everywhere needed toys to share with other children. Scholars needed exciting new books and the ability to understand them and explain them for the benefit of all. Skwoes everywhere needed points to buy clothes and food for Andillans caught up in their imaginings and disregarding their physical needs. Andillans were being so intensely generous in their mental creations for each other that they were running out of ideas of things to imagine and make happen, and yearned for new ones, mightily taxing Lenora's own imagination. So much need, so very much need.

Wanting filled Andilla, filled Lenora's mind. Her people cried out as one. It was almost more than she could bear, more than she could do.

But she loved them, she did, she really did love them, poor incomplete and inadequate beings. She could do it. She would do it.

"Lenora!" a voice said, momentarily distracting her from the destruction of all insects in a crop of the new hybridized purple mush to the south, the creation of a new kind of strawberry fudge brownie for Sayley, and the onset of world peace and universal brotherhood for a group of Andillans in search of an appropriate wedding gift for the coming celebrations.

It was Coren, her former love. He stood before her, his freckles shining in the golden glow of her love, his rather charming if merely human blue eyes gazing at her in adoration.

Simultaneously fulfilling hundreds and thousands of needs and desires all over Andilla, Lenora gazed back at him in wonder. He seemed to need nothing. Alone amid the hordes of wanting masses, he wanted nothing at all—nothing but to love her as he always had.

How good, how very good of him.

No, wait—he did want. She allowed herself to pay more attention to him, even though it was hard to do so and also do everything else demanded of her, required of her. Yes, she could feel the need emerging from him. Small, perhaps, but there.

Of course it was there. For all the charm of his eyes, he was just a mere measly human, pitiable and needy as the rest.

He needed a drink. He'd rushed all the way to come to her, and the hasty walking had made him thirsty.

Just a drink, a mere glass of water. Such a small thing.

Such a small thing—and there were people to feed, dragons to create, hairstyles to invent. Didn't he realize how busy, how very busy she was, how very many people needed her for so very many things? Couldn't he just go and get his own stupid glass of water?

Of course not, she thought to herself as she imagined the glass of water and placed it into Coren's waiting hand. He's just another human like all the rest. How very much they need me. How very little they deserve me, the puny little self-centered twerps.

She sighed, then went right back to fulfilling needs across the land. A cloud disappeared over a town to the south and reappeared over parched fields to the north. Sayley's tummy grew so large it actually pushed the table in front of it a few inches forward. Mud continued to be mud, but mud that was clean and did not ruin other people's clothing and could be packaged in convenient barrels and sold for a huge profit.

But wait. Lenora sensed that Coren was not satisfied yet. He still needed, still wanted, still demanded. Just like all the rest, all the thousands and thousands and thousands of imploring masses.

With growing anger, she looked into his mind and saw the picture he was imagining. The same drink. The same water, the same glass. But now there was a straw in it.

A *straw*? The poor little puny fool of a human wanted a *straw*? He wanted to enjoy sipping his drink daintily, through a stupid *straw*, of all things? Instead of just slurping it down sensibly and satisfying his stupid thirst?

"That's it!" she shrieked. "I've had it! I've completely and absolutely had it!"

The glow that emanated from her was changing color now, turning a rather lurid orange.

"You're just like all the rest of your puny, miserable breed," she shrieked into Coren's startled face, causing him to slop some of the water out of the glass. It splashed against her and immediately turned to steam in the growing heat of her glow.

"Always wanting! Always demanding! Always picking at me with your endless little petty desires! Never thinking of me or my needs! Pick, pick, pick, pick, pick! I've had it with you people! I've had it up to here!"

By now the glow had turned a bright fiery red. In the midst of it, Lenora's face was changing shape, becoming ugly and distorted.

"I hate you!" she shrieked, her nose growing longer and sharper and her eyes growing wider and redder. "I hate you all!"

And suddenly, her face disappeared altogether, replaced by a intense flash of fiery red light.

CHAPTER 25

In the midst of the flaming red light, a small black dot appeared and then began to grow. Soon it was a face—Hevak's face. It kept on growing. It floated gigantically and disproportionately over the top of Lenora's body like the head of some fantastic insect, hovering dangerously over the crowd gathered in the dining room to adore the wondrous Lenora and seek her favors. The blast of heat that emanated from it was so intense that it was almost unbearable. Some of the fresh new paint the Skwoes had applied began to scorch, and even Leni's remarkable hairstyle wilted.

"Lenora," the giant head wailed, its huge handsome mouth distorted in agony, its piercing eyes widened in horror. "We are one. We are great. We are good. Don't reject me. Don't push me out. Don't make me leave, oh, please don't make me leave! You want me, you do, you know you do. For you, for me, for all. We are one, we are, we are, we are one!"

But they were no longer one. Hevak's head separated from Lenora's body and floated up toward the ceiling like a monstrously disproportionate child's balloon. Below, in the midst of the angry flames that still poured from Lenora, her own face could be seen, confused, startled. She, too, looked up in wonder at the giant agonized head hovering over the room.

The head changed, began to thin out. Those looking up at it—anyone not busy stamping out the small fires that had developed in the carpet under their feet and in their own clothing—could see the ceiling right through it. The ceiling too was scorched black.

"You are choosing evil, Lenora," Hevak said, his voice growing hollow and echoing strangely. "Evil, evil! You're a good girl, Lenora, you are, you are. Remember the good. Please be a good girl, a good—"

But by now the voice had become so thin and hollow it could hardly be heard, and the head so cloudy it had almost disappeared from view altogether.

Almost, but not quite. As the crowd beneath watched, the remaining wisps of Hevak seemed to gather together right over Lenora's head and revolve around each other in an ever-tightening circle and an ever-quickening dance. They became a swirling tornado, a powerful vortex that seemed to pull all the color from the room below—and, fortunately, all the heat. As the fires went out and the light changed from red to orange, from orange to yellow, from yellow to mere ordinary daylight, Hevak's face appeared briefly again in the midst of the spinning vortex. Finally, the image whirled into nothingness. Hevak was gone.

Lenora looked up to where he had been in complete confusion. Then she turned her eyes downward and surveyed the room full of startled-looking people, smoke steaming up from various of their damaged garments. Then she looked at Coren, who still stood in front of her, a half-empty glass of water in his hand.

"Really, Coren," she said witheringly. "I don't know what's gotten into you. Be sensible for once. If you're all that thirsty, you don't have to wait for a straw."

EPILOGUE

Lenora raised her head from the toilet she was scrubbing and gave Coren a beseeching look. "This is awful," she said. "This cleaning stuff makes me gag. Couldn't I help it along just a little—like, disappear these pesky rust stains, maybe?"

"No, Lenora," he said from the ladder above her as he scraped at the peeling paint on the ceiling. "You promised. If you want to help me fix this place up, fine, you can help me. But no imagining. Not any. None. I made this room with my own two hands, and it's going to be fixed up that way if it takes us forever." He began scraping energetically once more, drizzling shreds of paint down onto Lenora's head and into the toilet.

Lenora sighed, picked some paint flecks off her brush, and began scrubbing again. It might well take forever at the rate things were going. And how could a little imagining hurt? If the rust stain was even just a teensy bit smaller—

"Lenora," Coren warned. "Don't even think it."

"Yes, Coren." As she replaced the rust to its former size, a new thought struck her. "Hey! How did you know I was thinking it? Have you been reading my thoughts again?"

"You bet I have."

I should have known, she thought, sending some particularly vile mental images of places he could go in his direction. Ever since the Andillan's powers had returned, Coren had been unable to resist using his. Having been deprived of them for so long, his entire attitude toward them had changed. "It was foolish of me to resist my nature," he had told Lenora. "I mean, sure, real painting and cleaning is fun—but I should have been proud of who I am and what I am."

Well, perhaps he should, even if it was more than a little annoying to have him rooting around in her private thoughts all the time. It seemed so unfair—Coren was now proud of his powers, but every time she used hers, even a little, the world nearly came to an end and she ended up with her head in a toilet.

"You're not being fair to yourself, Lenora," Coren said, still scraping. "It wasn't really your fault that Hevak came back. You can't be blamed for thinking a few good thoughts about making the world a better place and giving him a way back in again."

"I suppose not—except if it wasn't for me, Hevak wouldn't even have existed in the first place. He couldn't have come back because he just simply wouldn't have been."

"Look on the bright side. I mean, sure, things got pretty tense there for a while, but—"

"Pretty tense? I nearly goodied the entire known world into total subjection! All that awful goodness driving everyone completely crazy! And it was obviously Hevak showing up again that got everything unbalanced in the first place. What possible bright side can you see in that?"

Coren stopped scraping and put his hand on his chin, leaving paint smudges. "Well, let's see. For one thing, if Hevak hadn't shown up, we people here at the court would never have found out about the Skwoes—and the Skwoes wouldn't have found out more about us than they'd been willing to think about before."

"Yes," said Lenora, "that's true." Now that the people of

Andilla knew about each other, things were greatly improved for both the Skwoes and the court Andillans.

The Skwoes had the wonderful entertainment of cleaning and scrubbing the castle and all the other dilapidated courtier villages—and also, the huge profit in points they were making now that the Andillans had been forced to acknowledge the real state of their dwellings, outside of their perfect mental pictures of them, and had agreed to make point-laden contracts with the Skwoes to fix them up.

Meanwhile, the court Andillans were enjoying the benefits of the renovations. The castle had never looked better. Holes had been repaired, rotten staircases had been replaced with fresh wood, floors had been buffed, and now there was the smell of paint everywhere. Everyone's bruises and scratches were healing, and Queen Savet no longer had to worry about where her wedding guests would sleep or eat. In fact, a number of them had already arrived and were safely ensconced in comfortable, clean bedrooms hung with fresh wallpaper and filled with plenty of towels that had been crisply folded on the ingenious towel-folding machines Lenora had engendered for the Skwoes before Hevak had left her once more.

Nor was that all. Now that the two groups of Andillans knew about each other and had been forced to have interactions with each other, some of their qualities were beginning to rub off on each other. Lenora had actually overheard a conversation between Queen Milda and Sud Girth O60, in which Sud had asked what specific shade of blue paint he should use to carry out the cool, elegant look he was going for in the state throne room, and Milda had actually listened to him and then chosen an actual real paint chip.

Even poor little Mud had changed—possibly as a result of the broadening range of experiences Sayley continued to provide him with. In recent days, he had been a toad hopping in the cistern out behind the castle kitchens, a huge ugly pimple on the tip of Leni's nose (Sayley's way of killing two birds with one stone), a tiny speck of dust lost in a remote corner of the universe, and, for a few strange hours, nothing whatsoever at all.

"Which," Sayley had imperiously informed him, "is really what you are anyway."

But that was becoming less and less true. Mud was actually trying to have an imagination—perhaps, Lenora secretly thought, to make Sayley respect him a little more. He had found an old book of Coren's on the shelves in Cori's room called *Vocabulary for Fun and Profit*, and, after telling any Skwoe who would listen to him that being imaginative in your use of language was actually a major key to financial success and not impractical or counter-societal at all, he'd studied the book carefully and begun to intersperse his speech with his new discoveries.

"Sayley," Lenora once heard him say, "I abominate the methodology with which you continually insert your proboscis into my internal affairs. You owe me fourteen points."

"Oh, just dry up," Sayley said, and turned him into a small dust storm, which settled near the front door and was soon swept outside by a passing Skwoe.

Love, thought Lenora, works in mysterious ways.

In any case, the Balance had obviously changed in Andilla. The Skwoes were a little more like the courtiers, and the courtiers were a little more like the Skwoes. Everyone was a little more sensible as a result of it. Coren was right—that *was* a good thing. It was more—

More balanced, she told herself ruefully. Much as she hated to admit it, sometimes balance wasn't such a bad thing after all.

"Without it," Coren said, "I'd fall off this ladder and then where would you be?"

Ho, ho, she thought. "But seriously, Coren, look at how awful things got, just because Hevak tried to rid the world of evil."

"Yes," he agreed. "Just about as bad as they were when he tried to rid the world of good."

A new thought struck her. "Coren, what do you think has happened to Hevak?"

"I don't know," Coren sighed. "The important thing is, he's gone. We don't have to worry about him anymore."

Perhaps, Lenora thought—but then, that's exactly what we thought last time.

"Maybe so," Coren said. "But at least he's gone for now. Things are back to normal."

"More or less normal. There's Agneth to worry about." The Keeper had still not regained his mental balance, even though Kaylor spent hours with him every day, patiently reading to him from the Precious Records to soothe and heal his mind. He would sit calmly and nod in agreement, then suddenly get up and stand on his hands or turn a somersault.

"Yes," Coren agreed. "And my father hasn't quite recovered from his baking spree."

"And there's all those dead dragons out in the courtyard to deal with."

"Too true. That musclehead never knows when to stop, does he? There'll be enough dragon flambé for ten wedding banquets."

"And then there's Leni."

"Yes. If I were you, I'd stay out of her way for a while. She's still devastated about losing her moving hairdo."

Lenora smiled as she remembered the hairdo and all the other ingenious ways she'd fulfilled people's needs.

"I was good at being good," she said. "Wasn't I?"

"Too good," Coren agreed.

"But like you said, it's over."

Any day now, King Arno would discover fly fishing or stamp collecting or something and leave the kitchen forever. Any day now, Milda would have her full of dragon flambé and clear out the courtyard. Any day now, Leni would forgive Lenora because, as her mother had told her again and again, ladies don't hold grudges.

Any day now, Lenora and Coren could be married and be off to the private island. Any day now—because the monarchs had decided to delay the wedding until Agneth was in a proper state to perform the ceremony and bless the union. They didn't want the sacred rituals suddenly interrupted by a display of acrobatics.

But Agneth's somersaults were becoming increasingly infrequent. Agneth, too, would soon be back to normal. Soon, any day now, they could proceed with the wedding. Nothing, absolutely nothing, could stop it now.